Publisher:

FORTUNA PUBLICATIONS

www.fortunapublications.com

————————————

Editor:
Michael P. Roberts

————————————

Artistic Director:
Beverly A. Harris

————————————

e-mail address:
fortunapublications@gmail.com

We are soliciting for new stories and artwork to be featured in this magazine. If you have something for us to read or art to show, let us know by email.

EDITORIAL

Welcome to the second issue of **DETECTIVE MYSTERY MAGAZINE**.

We will be presenting a wide variety of detective and mystery stories from a variety of authors, new and old. If you have a story for us, please let us know.

We hope you enjoy this issue.

I0638022

HEADQUARTERS OF DETECTIVE MYSTERY MAGAZINE

Stories scheduled for upcoming issues include:

STOOGE FOR SLAUGHTER by W. T. Ballard
and other old and new stories

Murder in the Family was first published in 1943.
The Best Motive was published in 1953.
Bring Back a Corpse was first in 1956.
Alibi in Reverse was published in 1943.
Murder Among the Dying was published in 1945.

isbn 978-164720725

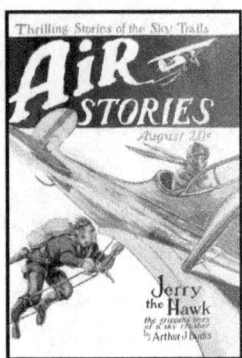

The Fiction House Press Replica Line is available at
www.FictionHousePress.com

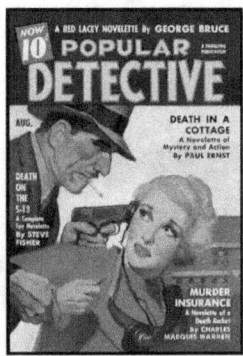

DETECTIVE MYSTERY MAGAZINE

CONTENTS

May 2020 Vol. 1, No. 2

Front Cover Illustration by Unknown

Published by Fortuna Publications

A girl's body was jammed between the stone tiger's jaws

IN THE FAMILY

By Leigh Brackett

*Everything was screwy; from the prehistoric
statues near the tar pits, to the whole Rieff family*

DANNY THAYER walked through the La Brea Tar Pits that night because he was looking for a place to sleep, free. He wasn't thinking about anything in particular. His brain had grown rather numb these last few days.

He was hungry. So hungry it felt like rats chewing inside of him. Maybe he could forget that, if he went to sleep.

Have to watch out for a cop, though. The signs at the park entrance said, "Closed to Public after Sundown."

The Pits stretched out before him, a great barren sweep of weeds and scrub and baked earth dotted with clumps of dark trees and the pits themselves where scientists had dug up fossils, and white scattered glints where stone sculptures of prehistoric

beasts loomed in the cloudy moonlight.

Danny Thayer shivered. He was nineteen, homeless, jobless, and hungry, but he could feel the loneliness of the place. It was more than just empty. It was—ancient.

Wilshire Boulevard was just beyond the wall of eucalyptus trees and ornamental shrubs. The lights of Hollywood painted the clouds off to his left. But they seemed a million miles away.

He walked on. Just walking, a tall lanky kid trying to forget how hungry he was. Past asphalt funnels bubbling stickily behind low protective walls. Past the statue of a short-faced bear, and two ground-sloths, and across a choked and stagnant creek.

The path led between pits choked with reeds higher than his head, over a low stone bridge. There was a thick clump of trees up ahead. The place had a sullen, biting smell. It seemed to be waiting, somehow. Waiting, and hungry.

Then, sharp and sudden in the dead silence, a woman's voice cried out.

"What are you doing? No! Oh God, don't . . .!"

And she screamed. It was a short scream, choked off abruptly in a sort of gurgle, like thick muddy water between stones.

Danny stopped. Something like a strong cold hand held him, still and not breathing. Then he started to run, toward the clump of trees ahead, his feet ringing hollow on the stone bridge.

He stumbled out of the path between the trees. The moon was playing hide-and-seek in drifting clouds. And someone was running, fast, toward the Wilshire entrance.

Someone in a dark suit, with a dark head bent. Running doubled over, so that in that light you couldn't see size and shape.

Danny Thayer yelled, almost as though his throat had done it alone.

The someone stopped, jerked around like a puppet on wires, already shadowed by the barrier trees. The moon broke out, clear and bright. For an instant they stood, the figure in the shadows, the boy clear in the cold brilliance. Then the dirt path was empty.

Danny stood still, his body needled with sweat, choking on his own heartbeats. The sullen pungence of the pits seemed suddenly triumphant, as though what they'd waited for had come.

He turned toward where the scream had come from.

There was a stone group under the trees, showing a bison mired in a pit and two sabre-tooth cats fighting over the carcass. One of them reared up over four feet, his head thrown back, fangs bared impotently while the other tore his throat.

Only now his fangs weren't bared. They were buried deep in a woman's throat.

A woman's throat, wedged with savage strength into the gaping mouth. The cat's fangs were metal, because they were too long for crumbly stone.

Metal. Not very sharp. But sharp enough.

CLOUDS nagged at the moon. Danny's heart beat full and slow and very loud. He shivered, and the veins in his neck hurt.

She was small and slender, bent backward and hanging from the cat's mouth. She wore an evening gown of some pale, shining stuff, tight across her small curved breasts. The blood had made a dark, glinting pool between them.

She must have been pretty, without her face so twisted and her eyes empty and staring. Her hair was dull gold against the stone.

It was very still and lonely there, and the pits smelt of death.

Danny put out his hands and tried to get her loose. But the curving fangs were hooked hard against her jaw. She was dead, anyway. Apart from the bleeding, the jerk of her body downward had snapped her neck.

He drew back. He wanted to be sick, but the retching was agony to the emptiness in him. And then he saw her purse, a little scrap of satin and seedpearls, dropped in the dust beside one small foot.

He stood quite still, looking at it. His bony hands opened and closed. He could still feel her flesh against his palms. Warm, but already cooling. Warm, but dead.

Just a dime, for a hamburger. It was stealing. But she wouldn't need it any more. Maybe it wasn't wrong to rob a person when he didn't need money any more.

Danny's jaw was long and jutting, covered with a dark soft stubble of beard. It set suddenly, hard, and his blue eyes narrowed.

"The hell with right or wrong! She's dead. And I'm hungry."

He stooped and caught up the purse and opened it. A roll of bills fell out into his hands. A thick, fat, solid roll of bills. Not the sort a girl carries in case of taxi fare.

Danny stood there, staring at it. And suddenly there was light in his face that wasn't moonlight, and a man's voice yelling.

Danny Thayer reacted from sheer brute instinct. He dropped the purse and lurched back into the shadow of the trees, and ran.

A whistle shrilled. Heavy boots pounded on the baked earth. A voice yelled, "Stop or I'll fire!" A prowl car must have stopped out on Curson Street, too far away for him to hear. The regular patrolman, clearing bums and lovers out of the park.

Danny ran. Fear lent him strength. Stumbling, staggering, doubled over with his back-muscles tight for the rip of a bullet, he raced around the pit where the bridge was, sheltered by the reeds.

He ducked in among the low walls. Something cracked like a dry branch behind him and there was a nasty whining sound over his head.

There were two sets of boots pounding, now. But the second cop, summoned by the whistle, was way behind.

The gun cracked again. Dust and splinters exploded from the wall beside him. It was hard to breathe, and his feet weren't sure.

He broke suddenly around a big pit with a sort of pump-house built over it, doubling back under the shelter of the tall cattails that choked the creek. The creek ran back almost to the Sixth Street side of the Pits. If he could make it . . .

The first policeman went into the tangle of low walls, carefully, lest Danny have a gun. Danny tried to go quietly, but he couldn't control his feet. His breath was hot and it had a sawedge to it.

The second policeman, way behind the first, saw him.

HE LET out a whoop and pelted across the shortened distance. He must have thought the boy was wounded, the way he was running, for he held his fire. Danny moaned and struck out for the shrubbery bordering Sixth Street.

The first man vaulted a wall and came running. Danny could hear their boots hitting the ground. They were going to run him down, because they were strong and not hungry. They were going to take him. They were going to arrest him for murder, because he'd been standing by a body with a purse in his hands.

Murder for robbery. Twelve men, and the gas chamber. And he didn't have even a description of the killer.

He was suddenly furious, the fury of an animal cornered and in pain. He grabbed up a big clod of earth and whirled around and threw it. His thin young lips were snarling, and his eyes were queer.

The leading policeman reached the creek. There was a gap in the reeds there, and he jumped. The clod took him, then, in the face. He lost his footing and crashed down, his head going under in strangling, acrid stuff, half water, half pure asphalt.

Danny ran on.

The other man yelled at him, and fired. Bullets kicked the dust, but he was weaving from sheer weakness, and the light was bad. They missed. He staggered into the shelter of the trees and looked back.

The cop had had to stop and pull his mate out of the creek. And now there were people coming into the pits from the Wilshire entrances, drawn by the whistles and the shots. He'd have to stay there, to guard the body and whatever clues there might be.

Danny Thayer stumbled on. No one was walking on Sixth Street at that hour, and the few cars went by fast. Nobody saw him, in the shadows. He went across into the grounds of a swank nursery, and then down on his knees in a dark corner, his breath knifing his lungs, his heart slamming his ribs like a hammer.

Far away a siren began to wail.

He had to get on. There'd be a cordon. He'd been a fool to run away. But his body did it without asking his mind, and then he'd been afraid to stop. Now nobody'd believe him.

But would they have believed him anyhow? A kid broke and starving, standing beside a dead girl with his fists full of money?

Money. Bills, a thick roll of them, clenched in his sweating hand. He'd taken it, then. Now they'd never believe him. Never.

Money. Something he'd prayed for, with his belly crying for food. Blood money, to buy him the gas chamber. He got up, whimpering, and raised his hand, as if to throw it away.

But he couldn't throw it away. It meant bus fare, to get away from here, quick. It might save his life. And it meant food. Just one full meal, before they caught him.

He began to rip feverishly at the bills. Got to hurry. Sirens. God, let them be small. Fives, tens, twenties. A lot of money. Why was she carrying it? A fiver. He pulled it out, and a scrap of paper fell at his feet.

He scooped it up and began to run again.

Out onto Wilshire Boulevard. Slowly, so as not to attract attention. Sirens, coming fast. Fairfax Avenue. There was a bus coming, heading toward Hollywood. People were beginning to stop and look for the sirens.

He sprinted across the intersection against the lights and caught the bus. The driver grumbled about changing the five, digging for dollar bills. The sirens screamed closer. Danny forced his hands to be steady, taking the change and dropping a dime in the box.

They started, jamming through on the caution light, the driver still sore about the change. They were in the last batch of cars through before the cordon closed around Wilshire and Fairfax.

THE bus was half empty. Danny sat by himself, trying not to sob when he breathed, trying to look peaceful. The roll fitted into his hand in his pocket, hard and accusing.

When they got as far north as Santa Monica Boulevard he began to relax a little. He got off there and went into a Log Cabin and ate. Then he took a red car and caught another bus on La Brea and went on to Hollywood. He went to three more drive-ins before he'd had enough to eat. He didn't dare have it all in one place, for fear of drawing notice.

Then he went out onto Sunset Boulevard, not knowing where to go next, or what to do. And for the first time he was really afraid.

He'd been afraid back at the Pits, with the hot animal fear of death. But this was different. This was being lost in a dark, cold place, where there was nothing but silence and waiting.

The night fog was coming in, chilly and smelling of the sea. It made little halos around the glare of Earl Carroll's. He could see people inside and hear music. The two big radio buildings across the street and the Palladium Ballroom radiated life and energy.

People, eating and drinking and having fun. Working. Fighting, maybe. But not afraid. Not behind a wall, like he was.

He sat down on a bench, shivering. The roll of bills made a lump against his thigh.

The policeman had seen him

pretty clearly by his flashlight. There'd be a description in the morning papers. They'd get him. They always got you.

The cop he'd hit wasn't dead, anyway. He'd moved and tried to get up when the other guy helped him.

If he could have caught the killer, or even seen his face. That girl, so little and golden-haired, with her throat ripped and jammed against those snarling fangs—and they thought Danny Thayer had done it!

How the killer must have hated her, to take her living throat in his hands and force it down. . . . What could a girl like that do to make anyone hate her so?

Surely, if he gave himself up, they'd know he couldn't have done a thing like that. But somebody might say, "You hated her because she had money and you were hungry, so you killed her."

Now he had money. Sure. Money. Money to buy the gas chamber.

It wasn't till then that he remembered the bit of paper.

It was still in his pocket. He spread it out under the lights from Earl Carroll's. Pencilled in a hasty, angry scrawl were the words, "This is all I can give you, ever, no matter what you do. Damn you, damn you, damn you!"

Danny turned the paper over. It was a strip torn from a department store sales slip. There was a name and address on it. Miss Cicely Rieff, who lived on Fountain Avenue.

The dead girl. She'd been taking that money to someone. Blackmail, sure as shooting. She must have been pretty desperate when she rolled the money up, to grab the nearest paper and scribble a note like that and wrap it in the heart of the wad.

Was the murderer the blackmailer? Maybe. The girl must have known him, to go into the Pits alone with him after dark. But why did he go off without his money, then? Had Danny scared him?

Danny Thayer, who was a fugitive from justice, with a roll of bills he couldn't spend. Danny, who was going to die in the gas chamber, unless . . .

Unless he could catch the murderer before the police caught him.

CHAPTER II

IT WAS almost as though his brain took hold and began to click without him, like a machine. He had clues—the note, the money, and the girl's name and address. He knew he wasn't the killer. That was more than the police had.

There hadn't been anything else in the girl's purse. Maybe it would take the police a little while to identify her. Until the morning papers came out, maybe, and somebody saw her picture.

It had been nearly ten when he found the body. It was nearly midnight now. Four or five hours he might hope for. Four or five hours to break into something from the outside and catch a killer.

It was hopeless, and he knew it. But it was better than just waiting, crouching in the dark with fear lying cold in his belly.

He'd still be in trouble, of course, even if a miracle happened and he did find the murderer. He'd do time for stealing and hitting a cop. But he could face that all right. It was the terrible fear of dying, for something he didn't do, that froze him.

He got up, thinking of the description the cop would give. There was a service station across the street. Nobody saw him go into the men's room and lock the door. He still had his cheap razor. Nothing for that in a hock shop.

He managed to scrape his face pretty clean, using just soap and water. Then he used the blade to chop his hair shorter. It looked ragged, but at least it was short. Then he did what he could to make his clothes look decent.

When he came out he looked different enough so that cops hunting for a shag-haired, unshaven kid wouldn't grab him straight off. He forced himself to walk with jaunty casualness, trying to keep in shadow without being too obvious about it.

It was well after midnight when he found the Fountain Avenue house.

It was one of those big old frame places—two stories and a half—left over from better days. A porch overgrown with bougainvillea ran around two sides. It was on a corner and there was a sign in the front bay window—ROOMS FOR RENT.

There were only one or two lights upstairs. That meant the police hadn't identified the body yet. If they had, the place would be blazing and full of people. He went around to the driveway. It led between high lattice fences, grown heavy with morning-glory vines, back to an old stable that was a garage now, with an apartment over it.

There were no lights in the back. Danny went softly down the drive. His heart was jumping like something trying to break loose.

The fog was heavier, but there was still moonlight. Everything was overgrown with vines and shrubs. It smelt musty and secret, and the lattice-covered back porch was a black hole with the garbage cans like ogre's eyes looking dully from under it.

He stood still by the corner of the house, then. He was here, but what next? He couldn't break into the house, yelling, "Who killed her?" The sharp chill of the air got inside him, and he felt the terrible, helpless weakness of an animal in a trap.

He went on, aimlessly, around the house. Noises came suddenly down to him from the garage apartment, so that he jumped and crouched trembling under a bush. A man's low thick laughter and a scuffling sound, and one sharp high titter in a woman's voice, and silence.

Danny crept on, still sweating with shock. He went along a dirt path between straggling flower beds, looking up at the dark house, wishing he were like Superman and could look right through walls.

Probably the killer wasn't here at all. If he was, there was no way to get at him. He might as well go and give himself up, now.

He didn't see the summer house until he almost ran into it. It was lattice like the fence, at the end of a pergola leading to a side porch. It was all choked with vines, smelling dusty and rotten in the damp night air.

And there were people inside.

A MAN'S voice spoke, right at Danny's shoulder, just beyond the vines. A low voice, smooth and drawling and soft, and somehow worse than if it hadn't been.

"I just want to know where she is, Frieda."

"I tell you I don't know!" It was a woman this time, breathless, frightened, almost crying. "I haven't any control over Cicely."

"Very well, Frieda," said the man pleasantly. "I'm in no hurry."

"I don't understand." The tone of the woman's whisper did something to Danny's insides. "Teddy, if you've harmed her . . ."

"Why should *I* harm Cicely? Just because Mother doesn't love her darling niece?" There was a rustle of swift movement and a sharply indrawn breath.

"Don't, Teddy! It hurts!"

The man said silkily, "Does it? I'm glad. Just remember it, in case . . . What's that? There's someone outside!"

Danny got up and ran. A big moth had blundered suddenly into his face, so that he jerked his head and struck the vines and rustled them. He dodged into the shadows of a big tree and around it to the garage, where steps came down from the apartment.

Feet were running close behind him. He knew he'd have nightmares about running feet all the rest of his life. He'd slip behind the garage to the street, and then . . .

There was no way behind the garage, and the fence was too high to get over in time. He was caught.

He turned, then, his bony young face snarling, his fists balled. Scared, and angry because he was scared, and furious suddenly with fate for picking on him. A tall slender man in slacks and a sport coat was almost on him, running gracefully, like a dancer.

Danny lashed out at a smooth blond head, missed because the head moved aside a fraction, and felt something crash below his left ear.

He went sprawling, the breath knocked out of him against hard ground. A hand gripped his collar, dragged him upward, strangling, and then knuckles slashed him twice across the mouth.

The darkness turned suddenly red. Danny made an animal noise and doubled his feet up and kicked. The blond man grunted and lurched back, his handsome face twisted like a fiend's in the moonlight.

The girl cried out sharply, then. She'd been a long way behind the man. Now she got between him and Danny, and said rapidly:

"Wait, Teddy! Don't! It's my friend Dick Taylor, from back home."

Teddy scowled down at her, his fists clenched and showing blood on the knuckles. "You're lying," he said.

"I'm not, I swear it! Dick, you tell him I'm not. Dicky!"

Danny's brain was numbed with anger and pain and wondering if the girl was crazy. Almost without thinking, he mumbled, "Sure I'm her friend. Who'd you think I was—Hitler? Hi, Frieda."

Lucky he'd heard her name. Teddy stood irresolute, swinging his fists in little tight arcs, like a cat swings its paws. And then the door opened, up above at the head of the stairs.

A MAN came out. He was wearing a big coat and carrying his hat, and his feet stumbled on the wooden platform He said thickly, "G'nigh', Princess. Thursday, huh?" He chuckled and turned, and then he saw the group at the foot of the stairs.

Danny saw his face for one stricken moment. Then the man slammed his hat on and pulled it hard over his face and ran down the stairs, hanging onto the rail and stumbling until Danny thought he'd fall. He shoved past with his head down and went lurching down the drive.

Danny knew who the man was. He made a lot of money, kissing pretty women for the movies.

A woman came out of the door upstairs. She wore a thin silk robe, and she was a looker. She leaned over the rail, with her dark hair hanging over her shoulders, and blew a long plume of smoke. Her voice was tired and bored.

"What goes on?"

"Nothing," said Frieda. "Just a friend of mine from back home. He hitch-hiked all the way out here, and

then Teddy . . ."

Teddy's voice was sullen, but still smooth. "What's he doing prowling in the yard at this time of night?"

Danny's brain had been churning furiously. The girl must have her reason for this. And it gave him his chance to get inside. The least he could do was play up to her.

He got up, wiping the blood off his chin, and said, "Trying to get hold of Frieda. I'm broke, and I didn't think the landlady would let me in, the way I look. Sure quick with your fists, aren't you?"

"Quick," said Teddy softly, "and accurate."

The woman in the silk robe came down the stairs, her slipper heels clicking. Her legs showed white against the darkness.

"Spoils," she said bitterly, and let something glitter in her hand. "Now I'll go find the old highbinder."

"The intricate pattern of crime," said Teddy, almost absently. "So much more fascinating than a jigsaw puzzle. Isn't it, Frieda?"

Frieda didn't say anything. Danny had his first real look at her. She wore something plain and dark, and she wasn't very tall. Her hair was the color of wheat, falling loose on her shoulders.

He thought her eyes were blue, but in that light all he knew was that they had hate in them. Hate, and fear, looking at Teddy.

"Come on, Dick," she said. "I'll get you a room."

He followed her. Out in the street a motor roared and coughed, as though someone were in an awful hurry to get away. And a light went on in the second story, as though the motor was a signal.

Teddy laughed behind them, a soft nasty little sound. The woman in the silk robe plodded up into the black hole of the porch. And Frieda shrank suddenly against Danny and cried, "What's that?"

There was something sprawled in the shadows of a clump of hydrangeas. Danny hadn't seen it before. But the moonlight had shifted a bit, and one white hand showed up against the grass.

A man's hand, lying across the dull metal of a gun.

They went to it, not speaking at first. Teddy knelt down and rolled the body partly over by the shoulder. The woman in the silk robe made a little choked scream and came back, her heels scuffing.

"It's Halstead," said Teddy. "Somebody's knocked him on the head."

Frieda said, in a queer flat whisper, "My God. Who would want to kill poor Mr. Halstead?"

Teddy's eyes were slanted like a cat's, glinting in the moonlight. He pointed to the gun. "Who did poor Mr. Halstead want to kill? Can't guess, can you, Frieda?"

Frieda pressed tight against Danny, so tight he could feel the roll of bills in his pocket digging into her. She shivered and said wearily, "Haven't you any heart at all?"

The woman gripped her thin robe together at the throat. "I'm getting out of here. The other I'm used to, but

murder . . !"

Teddy got up, dusting his knees. "No use, Princess. The police don't like the contestants running out on their quiz shows."

Policemen. Policemen coming from one murder to another and finding Danny Thayer. There wouldn't be any time, now. They'd recognize him. Frieda would admit her lie. And if he ran away . . .

He was scared. Cold inside, and scared, and kind of dazed, like an animal when it finds the steel jaws in its leg are there to stay.

THE porch door opened. A woman's harsh whisper said, "Get in here, you fools! Want everybody . . . My God, what's that!"

"A corpse, Mother," said Teddy. "Your late boarder, Mr. Halstead." There was a malicious, concealed amusement in his easy voice.

The porch door shut. A woman scuffed heavily out from under the shrouding vines and down the steps as fast as her heavy bulk could make it. Her frizzed white hair stuck out, quilled here and there with curlers. When she came across the wet grass she pulled up the straggling skirts of her nightgown and flannel wrapper, and Danny saw her ankles, thick and white and bunchy with veins.

"He must have had a heart attack," she said. "A heart attack. His heart was weak, you know." Then she saw the gun and stopped, her breath wheezing in her thick throat. "Suicide?"

"He hasn't been shot. And I don't think he cracked his own skull."

Danny saw the cat-glitter of his eyes, studying the woman, laughing.

"We'll have to call the police," said Frieda. Teddy shot her a bright, hard look, and smiled. He was handsome, like a blond Satan.

The fat woman said rapidly, "No, wait. Maybe he cut himself falling. Let's get him inside—" Then she saw Danny. Her voice went suddenly ugly. "Who's this?"

"I'm a pal of Frieda's, from back home." Her eyes were like small hard pebbles, staring right through Danny. They made him tighten inside. But she was scared, too. She didn't want the police. If he could bluff this through, hang onto his chance. . . .

Her face was like a coarse, evil mask of stone in the moonlight. Danny could sense her thoughts running like rats behind it. Then she said, "All right. Grab hold of his feet and help Mr. Rieff."

Teddy Rieff. The dead girl had been his cousin, then. Danny got the corpse around the knees. Everything was quiet. The people in the front hadn't heard. The dead man was heavy, and his clothes were damp. Teddy pocketed the gun.

They went in through the dark porch, to a stale-smelling kitchen. A night light burned in the hall beyond. They went toward it, as quietly as they could, across a bare, creaky wooden floor.

They were almost there. And then a door opened suddenly, right at Danny's shoulder, so that he almost dropped the body. Dim light from the hallway outlined a woman's head

against the darkness.

Hair flattened in wet curls under a net, with a face the shape of a pear sagging out from under it, a wide weak mouth and eyes that popped a little. Eyes that were wide open and staring, fixed on the dead man's bloody face, lolling back against Teddy's stomach.

CHAPTER III

SHE didn't speak. Danny didn't know how long they stood there. Then Mrs. Rieff said sharply,

"Go to your room, Princess. I'll see you later."

Princess went out, holding her silk robe away as she passed the corpse. And Mrs. Rieff moved, very quickly for a heavy woman.

Her right hand clamped just above the staring woman's elbow. Her left smothered the whimpering cry of pain. She whispered savagely,

"You know about this, Millie, don't you?" Her fingers tightened. The woman strained away, her pale eyes stretched with fear.

"Tell me," said Mrs. Rieff softly, "or you'll get no nights off for six months."

The woman made a strangled whining sound and tried to nod. Mrs. Rieff took her hand away. Millie started to speak, her mouth open as though once started the stream of words wouldn't stop.

"Not here!" snapped Mrs. Rieff, and shook her viciously. "Upstairs, and be quiet!"

Down a dingy hall and up back stairs that must have been worked on lately, because they didn't creak, Mrs. Rieff opened a door and motioned them in, listened a minute, and then came after them.

Lamps made a subdued purplish light. Danny guessed it was Mrs. Rieff's room. There were photographs and expensive knicknacks all over the mantel and the tables. It was all crowded and choked and overdone.

He helped Teddy Rieff put the body down on a couch. Mr. Halstead had been a kindly-looking man, grey-haired and tired. There was a bruise and a big cut on his face.

Danny straightened up, waiting. He put his hands in his pockets to steady them, and the roll felt big and hard, like a judge's hammer when he passes sentence.

He saw Frieda looking at him. A queer, desperate look. And then Mrs. Rieff's pebble eyes were fixed on him.

Her face was coarse and puffed, with red broken veins under the skin. Danny was afraid of her, suddenly. She said sharply,

"So you're a friend of Frieda's, eh?"

"Sure. My name's Dick Taylor. I hitch-hiked out here, and landed broke. I wanted to get hold of Frieda first. I didn't think you'd let me in, the way I look. I . . ."

"Well, you're in now." There was something terrible in the slow, reflective way she said it. "Frieda, where's Cicely?"

"I don't know." She was pretty, now that you could see her face. She looked tired and sort of stony. Danny felt suddenly protective.

Mrs. Rieff smiled. It was like Teddy's smile, catlike, malicious and secret. She turned suddenly on the staring, pale-eyed woman.

"All right, you, Millie. What about this?"

Millie licked her lips. She seemed drugged and dazed with fear. She stood utterly still, her big rough hands hanging, staring at the sprawling corpse. She wore bright green silk pajamas and a pink wrapper and pink slippers of quilted satin.

Her mouth worked for a long time before the words came, ragged and tumbling.

"I was coming back from the trashpile. I saw him, hiding in the bushes, He was waiting . . ."

"What were you doing at the trashpile at that hour?"

"I—please, Mrs. Rieff, I only took two slices. Don't!"

Mrs. Rieff did, with relish. "Stealing bacon again, and trying to hide the grease. Well, stop rubbing your stupid face. Go on."

Millie's pale, protruding eyes swung again to the body.

"He had a gun," she whispered. "He looked sick. He told me to go away, but I knew what he was doing. He was waiting to kill Miss Cicely. I heard him tell her he would, if she didn't let him alone."

Her big rough hands knotted together suddenly. "He wouldn't stop. So I hit him with the skillet, on the head. He—he made a funny choking noise and fell down. I was scared. I ran, inside . . ."

Millie crumpled slowly down to her knees, staring straight ahead of her, her hands loose in her lap.

"I didn't mean to kill him," she said dully. "I only didn't want him to hurt Miss Cicely. She's kind to me. She's the only person that ever was kind to me. She gives me pretty things, and money enough to go to two movies on my night off."

She looked up then, with something bright and burning in her eyes.

"You all hate her," she said. "You all wish she was dead. But she's kind to me. And no one's going to hurt her, if I can help it!"

She relaxed, as though there was nothing left in her, and just sat there, tears running silently down her flabby cheeks.

Teddy had been bending over the body. He spoke now, rapidly.

"I DON'T think this whack was hard enough to kill him, Mother. Stunned him, probably, and he raked his face on the bushes, falling. The old boy had a weak heart. Probably the strain of planning the murder, and getting caught, and the blow, brought on a fatal attack."

Mrs. Rieff looked down at the body with hard, narrow eyes.

"So Cicely was blackmailing him, eh? Clever girl. Let that be a lesson to you, my son. Only a genius would have looked for profit in that dried-up old priss!"

She laughed suddenly, a startling wheeze of private mirth, and settled heavily into an overstuffed chair.

"Get up, Millie. Go to bed. And if you open your mouth about this, I'll swear you killed him. Just forget Mr. Halstead, Millie. And you can forget your night off this week, too, so you'll remember the bacon."

Millie said, "Then I didn't really kill him?"

"No. But I can swear you did. Now go and dream of Clark Gable."

Millie got up. She looked at Mrs. Rieff with dumb, weary hate, like a beaten animal, and went. Mrs. Rieff said briskly.

"That's that. We'll forget about the gun. Halstead had a heart attack and hurt his head falling. We brought him in, but it was too late. Teddy, you and the kid carry him to his room and then call a doctor. Make all the noise you want to. We want witnesses."

She got up and took the gun out of Teddy's pocket and wiped it carefully. Then she pressed Halstead's stiffening fingers on it, in several places, wrapped it in a handkerchief, and gave it back.

"Stick it in one of his drawers. If he had a license they'll look for it. If he hasn't, well, we don't know anything about it."

She looked at Danny, with her hard, flat pebble eyes, and said, "Then you can have Number Eight, here in the rear. Any friend of my niece's—we don't want you to get away too soon."

Teddy smiled. "Welcome to our happy home. Grab his feet again."

Danny did. Frieda started out with them, but Mrs. Rieff said, "Stay here, dear. Two of them is enough."

Frieda shot him a veiled, urgent look and stopped, reluctantly. They went on with the body, through a door that closed the back part of the hall off from the front. They made a lot of noise. Presently there were people swarming around, talking, questioning, staring.

They got Halstead into his room. Teddy palmed the gun somehow and got somebody busy calling a doctor and went out again with Danny. Danny was only vaguely conscious of what went on. His brain was spinning like a squirrel in a cage, and making about as much progress.

The things he had found out, instead of simplifying the problem, had only made it harder. Cicely Rieff had been a blackmailer. The servant said everybody hated her. Halstead had been driven to murder.

Who else in this house was Cicely blackmailing? And who had been blackmailing her? And what about?

Frieda, who must be Cicely's sister, was afraid of Teddy Rieff. Why? And was there really some pleased and secret knowledge in Mrs. Rieff's eyes, or had he just imagined it?

The girl Frieda was the pivot. If he could be alone with her . . .

TEDDY RIEFF closed the hall door behind them. "The Great Divide," he chuckled. "The back is strictly family territory. The boarders even have to garage their cars elsewhere, and there are no keys to the back door given out."

His slanting cat-eyes were fixed sharply on Danny. "Therefore you are the first outsider to see what you have seen."

He meant about the apartment over the garage. Danny grinned. "I know how to keep quiet. Say, I'd like to see Frieda before I turn in. Been a long time, and we were pretty chummy."

"Sure," said Teddy. "Four years is a long time. How are things back in Kansas?"

"About the same," said Danny warily. Teddy stopped before a door and opened it, snapping the light on inside.

"This is your room, kid. Suit you?"

"Sure, anything." He wanted to see Frieda, alone—and quick. A siren wailed suddenly over on Sunset, and his guts knotted tight inside him. But it went by. He started off down the hall.

He didn't even have time to turn. The swift movement behind him melted right into the chopping blow on the side of his neck. His heart seemed to close up on him, and his body just folded, heavily.

He didn't quite go out. He felt Teddy's arms like lean steel cables around him, and knew dimly that he was dragged and lifted and stretched on something. He began to struggle then, glaring up at Teddy in a sort of dazed fury.

But it was too late. He was spreadeagled on the bed, tied wrist and ankle to the brass posts. Teddy smiled down at him.

"Frieda's only been out here two years," he said gently, "and she came from Michigan. Better start talking, kid."

The blood thundered in Danny's head. It hurt, and he couldn't think. He whispered, "You go to hell."

"Inevitably. But not just yet," Teddy's long fingers twisted cruelly in Danny's hair, lifting his head. "What's between you and Frieda? Something about Cicely?"

Danny wasn't afraid now. Just mad. He thrashed his head about and tried to bite Teddy's wrist. Teddy laughed and slapped him, just hard enough to make his ears ring.

"Okay. We'll do it the hard way." He whipped his handkerchief tight around Danny's jaws to keep him from yelling, and went through his pockets.

Then he stood silent for a long minute, looking at the roll of bills and the crumpled paper with the note and the address on it.

HE POCKETED them at last, slowly, and bent over Danny again. His handsome face had deep, cruel lines in it.

"She's dead, then."

Danny nodded. No use trying to hide that any longer. Teddy ripped off the gag.

"What do you know about this?"

Danny burst out, "Nothing! I was just walking through the Tar Pits, looking for a place to sleep. I heard a woman scream, and saw someone running away. Then I found the body, and the money and then the cops found me. They think I did it."

"They do!" said Teddy softly. His hand closed on Danny's shirt collar, pulled him up ruthlessly to the reach of his bound arms. Teddy's cat-eyes were pale and cold and yet somehow blazing. He said, "Did you see the killer?"

"Only someone running."

"Man or woman?"

"Someone in pants. Dark hair."

"Dark hair. You're sure of that?"

Danny looked at the light shining on Teddy's smooth blond head. "You could have worn a cap," he said grimly.

Shot in the dark. He shivered, looking at Teddy's face.

Teddy laughed. A soft, secret little laugh. "Yes. I could, couldn't I?" He let Danny down again and replaced the gag.

"Just lie still, little one. Daddy has business to attend to. Oh, yes. Big, important business. And I need you!" The lights went out. Teddy opened the door and closed it softly behind him, and Danny Thayer was alone.

He lay there with the blood pounding in his bruised neck, his legs and arms beginning to ache where they were tied, and thought, "He did it. He did it, and he's going to pin it on me."

His brain began to click over again, like a well-oiled engine. What motive could Teddy Rieff have for killing his cousin Cicely? Well, Cicely was blackmailing at least one other person so that he was willing to murder her. Why not Teddy, too? Or Teddy's mother?

Teddy's mother. That apartment over the garage, Princess, and the prominent actor. Mrs. Rieff was prosperous. Boarding-house keepers don't get that way solely from the boarders, and women who run small apartments over garages don't get that way splitting diamond bracelets with the girls. There's another, quicker way . . .

Blackmail. You always came to blackmail in this house. Ten to one Mrs. Rieff blackmailed the men who came to the rear apartment. She'd want to keep her skirts clean, though, in case of trouble. She took plenty of precautions. It wouldn't be easy to get anything on her.

But suppose somebody did. Wouldn't she rather split her profits than be exposed or give the whole thing up?

All right. Say Cicely Rieff, her niece and therefore admitted into the family circle, had proof of Mrs. Rieff's business and blackmailed her with it. Remembering Mrs. Rieff's heavy face and hard pebble eyes, Danny didn't think she'd take it too long. She'd get busy figuring out a way to rid herself of the blackmailer.

She wouldn't do it herself. She'd delegate someone else. And who better than her son, Teddy? Just like, a few minutes ago, she had said, "We don't want you to get away too soon," and Teddy had smiled . . .

Perhaps Frieda Rieff knew too much. Perhaps that was why Teddy had threatened her in the summer house.

Danny groaned. Just guessing wouldn't do him any good. He had to have proof. Time, the little time he had, was rushing by. And here he was, trussed up and waiting.

Waiting. Remembering Teddy's long sinewy hands, Danny shuddered. And then, very softly, somebody opened the door.

CHAPTER IV

DANNY lay quite still, hardly breathing. His nails dug into his palms, but he didn't feel them. He watched the dark huddled bulk come in, saw the door swing shut again, and listened to feet scuffing stealthily across the carpet.

A match flared and sputtered startlingly, close to his face. And Millie's voice, hushed to a hoarse whisper, asked, "Are you all right?"

All the strength poured out of Danny's rigid body. He said shakily, "Sure. Untie me, quick. What are you doing here?"

The match went out. He could feel her rough fingers fumbling at his wrists. Her voice came raggedly, as though some great pent-up emotion in her forced it out against a barrier of fear.

"Miss Frieda sent me. She upset a vase on her dress, so she could get away from the old woman for a minute to change it, and she sent me up here. She thought they were going to do something to you. She needs your help. That's why she lied about knowing you."

Millie's voice broke in a dry sob. "I heard through the wall, waiting in the next room for Teddy to go away. Poor Miss Cicely! She knew they wanted to kill her. She was afraid. I know she wasn't bad! She was kind to me, and I loved her."

She had one wrist free and started on the other. Teddy had tied hard knots in the handkerchiefs he used. Her voice stumbled on.

"I heard Mr. Halstead threaten her yesterday, and the old woman was in a black fury all day. I know Cicely was asking for more money, and I know she was in trouble. She hasn't been herself ever since Frieda had to go back to Michigan on business, four months ago.

"I wanted to help her. But she'd never tell me what was wrong. Anyway, there was nothing I could do. There—never has been."

Wrists free, and both of them working on ankles lashed tight with leather belts, Millie's shaken voice went on again.

"She was frightened, I tell you. She gave me three dollars this morning, and then she said, 'This may be the last money I'll ever give you, Millie. If anything happens to me, Frieda—' And then Mrs. Rieff came into the kitchen and she stopped.

"I think she was going to say that Miss Frieda would give me things. I don't think so. She's a nice girl, but she lives inside herself so much. But I don't care about that. I loved Miss Cicely. She's the only person I ever had to love."

Danny was glad it was dark. He hated to see women cry. He said, "Why haven't you left this place, or called the police?"

"I didn't have anything to call the police about. The old woman's careful about that. I'd only have gotten Princess and Miss Cicely in trouble.

Besides—" She helped him off the bed, and he could hear her throat working, trying to keep the terror and the tears in check.

"Besides, I didn't have anyplace else to go. I'm not young. It isn't easy to find a place these days. Mrs. Rieff knows that, and she knows I'm too dumb and too scared to fight her."

Her voice dropped suddenly to a strange tight whisper. "Only this time I'm not. They've killed Cicely, she and her wicked son. They've killed her. And I'm not going to let them get away with it!"

Danny said awkwardly, "Come on, then. We'll get Frieda."

His hand was on the knob when Millie's fingers closed sharply on his wrist. He heard them, then. Slow, heavy footsteps, coming closer.

"The old woman," whispered Millie. "Maybe she's coming to make sure."

They waited. No time, no place to hide or get away. There was sweat on Danny's temples. The footsteps stopped outside the door. He could hear her heavy breathing beyond the thin panel.

The knob turned in his fingers.

THE barrier door down the hall opened, and a voice said, rather timidly, "The doctor's here, Mrs. Rieff."

She said, "All right," and let go of the knob and went on. Danny's knees sagged. He waited until the outside door closed, and went out.

There was nothing in the hall but silence and the dim glow of the night light, until they reached the door of

Mrs. Rieff's room. There were voices behind that, low but not very guarded, as though they were sure of not being overheard.

Frieda's voice, tight and shaken, saying, "What a filthy trick! You were blackmailing your own mother."

"Naturally. Lucrative work, if you can get it. Of course, I knew it wouldn't last forever. That's why I kept asking for more, and Cissy had to shake more out of the victims in order to meet all her—er—obligations. Naturally, the victims began to kick. The last raise was just the final spur."

He laughed. "This will be a shock to mother. She trusts my filial devotion so completely!"

"And that boy?"

"That boy," said Teddy softly, "is going to be a scapegoat. I'm going to tie all his little curiosities to his horns and run him straight back to the police—dead."

There was a queer sharp edge to Frieda's voice, a stillness. "And what about me?"

"Now that this game is played out, I'm thinking of taking over Mother's business and enlarging it. I want . . ." He seemed to move closer to the girl, and his voice dropped so that Danny couldn't hear.

Frieda's voice came suddenly, sharp and harsh. "No! You devil, I won't do it! Teddy, you . . . oh!"

Danny said quietly, "Millie, go phone the police. I'm going in there."

He still had no direct, incriminating evidence. Teddy's implied confession wouldn't be enough to condemn him. But Danny figured he'd have at least a chance this way. And he couldn't let Teddy just go on. Cicely had already died. Frieda might be next.

Millie gripped his arm tight. "Be careful—and I hope this'll mean the rope for both of 'em!"

She went off down the hall, almost running, her bright green pajamas flapping around her thin legs. Danny, very quietly, opened the door.

They didn't see him come in, for a moment. Teddy had his back to Danny, his hands on Frieda's arms below the shoulders. She had changed into a dark blue wrapper with a long gold arrow on the collar. She was straining away from him, her eyes blazing out of a face white and hard as scraped bone.

Teddy murmured, "You'd be a pretty woman, Frieda, if you weren't such a blasted martinet!"

She said something, so low and hissing that Danny couldn't get it. Then she saw him, coming up behind Teddy. Her blue eyes widened.

Teddy turned swiftly, his handsome face startled and wicked as a blond Satan. Frieda cried out, "Help me! Please help me!"

Danny said evenly, "I'm just waiting for the chance."

It was the first time in his short life he'd ever felt real hate.

HE WENT in on Teddy Rieff, watching the poise of his blond head, the swing of his fists and shoulders. His first blow just grazed Teddy's jaw. He twisted to take the counterblow on his shoulder, crouched, and slashed upward.

His fist smashed into a belly tight and hard as board. It jolted both of them. Then a roundhouse swing connected with Danny's ear. He went down, grabbing at Teddy's knees, pulling him off balance and into a table loaded with china and glass.

It went over with a crash. Frieda had closed the hall door and was standing flat against it, watching with wide, bright eyes. Teddy cut his hand on a broken vase, and there began to be red splashes over the rug and Danny Thayer.

There wasn't much science to it. Danny just hung on, punching, kicking, grappling. Teddy was heavier and experienced. Danny's long rangy frame hadn't reached its real strength yet. But Danny had made up his mind to one thing.

This time he wasn't going to be licked.

Teddy's knee ground agonizingly into his belly. Hard knuckles slashed and pounded at his face. His mouth was full of blood and his ears roared. He set his teeth and twisted like an eel, grabbing out blindly.

He got Teddy by the shirt collar. The cloth was stout. Danny's arm was long, and his position gave him leverage. He dragged Teddy over, heaving his body underneath to break his balance. His eyes were swelling and full of blood, but he could feel.

He twisted the collar tight, working his fingers like a bulldog's jaws, in and in, his head sunk and his back humped to take Teddy's blows.

Teddy swore, viciously, between his teeth. He was dragging at Danny's wrist now, but Danny's long bony fingers were tangled in the cloth, twisting, twisting. Teddy lurched back and up, shaking himself.

Danny kicked at his ankles and brought him down again, hard. He got his other hand on the collar and his knee on Teddy's right arm. Teddy's left hand raged at his face, clawing. Danny put his head deep between his shoulders to save his eyes, and then Teddy found his ear.

Danny screamed, and Teddy laughed, a sort of strangled gurgle. Danny flung himself downward suddenly. Teddy's nails slipped out of his ear. His right arm came free as Danny's knee moved with his body.

Danny lay flat on top of Teddy, grinding his fingers in, twisting the cloth tighter and tighter. He could feel the hard, straining cords of Teddy's throat, the softer spot beneath the Adam's apple. He began to get scared. He didn't want to kill.

Teddy's nails were ripping his shirt and the flesh under it. He tore away suddenly and loosed one hand from Teddy's throat and brought it crashing down against his temple.

Teddy's hands faltered. Danny flailed his fist down twice more. Teddy Rieff lay still, breathing hoarsely through his mouth.

Danny got up. Very slowly, waiting for the pain to break through the numbness. Through a wavering red curtain he saw Frieda.

"Tie him up," he said thickly. "Keep him. Police . . ."

The golden arrow on her collar

flashed at him. "Police?"

"Coming. Millie sent for them. Teddy killed your sister . . ."

"Yes," she said. "Yes. I know that. Are you all right?"

"I guess so." He wiped the blood out of his eyes and swallowed what was in his mouth. Teddy was groaning on the floor. Danny said, "We'll have to take care of his mother somehow. Lock the door, maybe. Keep her out till the police come."

Frieda nodded and turned the key. Teddy looked awful, bloody and choking on his breath. It scared Danny. What if Teddy died?

He was Danny's only proof of innocence. There was no direct evidence against him. But the police would at least investigate, might find some, might even force him to confess.

But with Teddy dead, at Danny's hands. . .

HE WASN'T dead. He was tough. A little blood didn't mean much. Danny pulled himself together and helped Frieda tie him with curtain cords.

Then he just sat, looking across at Frieda. Her hair looked even paler against the dark blue robe, gold and shining like the arrow on her collar. Her eyes were very blue. She smiled tremulously, and said,

"This is what I prayed you'd do. I've been so frightened. My sister—wasn't good to me, and Teddy . . . I didn't know anyone to ask help from, and when you came, I—you might have been killed. Can you ever forgive me?" He waved a bruised hand awkwardly. "You gave me my chance. The cops think I killed your sister."

"Teddy told me about that."

"How did the old woman let herself get blackmailed?"

Frieda shrugged wearily. "Cicely's been working on it ever since we came out here to live with Aunt Grace. Our parents died, you see. Cicely never told me much, but I think she got a candid camera shot of Aunt Grace—Mrs. Rieff—taking a necklace from Princess. It didn't mean much by itself. But Cicely had a case all built up in her mind, enough so that my aunt didn't want to risk an investigation."

She caught her breath suddenly, looking toward the door. "She's coming back."

Danny got up and went to the door. Fear began to knot his insides again, he didn't know why. She was a woman, and locked out. But there was something about her, about her eyes . . .

Her heavy footsteps came up and stopped outside, and for the second time that night the knob turned under Danny's fingers. He said, "The door's locked, Mrs. Rieff. It's going to stay locked until the police get here."

There was a startled intake of breath, and a silence. Then her voice came, ominously quiet.

"Have you hurt Teddy?"

"He'll be all right. Only he's staying here, for the police."

And then, sharp and taut behind him, Frieda screamed.

Danny whirled around. Frieda was half crouched over Teddy, her hands pressed over her heart. She looked up at him, slowly.

"He's dead," she whispered. "You've killed him."

Danny went forward, three wavering, leaden steps. Teddy lay utterly still, not groaning, not breathing. His lips were blue. Mrs. Rieff called from beyond the door, but Danny hardly heard her.

He stood staring down at the body. His bony hands opened and closed slowly, still feeling Teddy's living throat against them.

Teddy's throat. Cicely's throat. They'd never believe him now. "Frieda. Frieda!"

The girl looked at him, dazed.

"Frieda, you'll tell them how it happened. You'll tell them . . ."

She crumpled down gently at his feet, lying like a tired child with her cheek on her hand, the arrow glinting on her breast.

It was then that Mrs. Rieff came in. There must have been another door into the hall. She came slowly through the bedroom door to Danny's right. She carried a snub-nosed automatic, with a silencer on it.

CHAPTER V

HER eyes were like small polished bits of steel, sunk deep under heavy lids, seeing everything. Teddy's battered body. Blood splashed over the carpet. Danny, standing on widebraced feet, beaten and torn and half stripped, wild with numb terror. And Frieda, lying quiet, her wheat-gold hair burning against the rug.

Without speaking or letting the automatic waver a fraction of an inch, Mrs. Rieff bent down and put her free hand on Teddy's throat, feeling for the pulse under the jaw. Then she pulled back an eyelid and gave one swift, keen look. She got up. Her heavy face was almost expressionless, but Danny's heart twisted in him like a scared animal.

He whispered, "I didn't mean to kill him."

"That's too bad." Her voice, held tight to a level, throaty whisper, betrayed what she was feeling. "That's too bad!"

Time, the room, the universe, shrank in on Danny Thayer so he could hardly breathe. The focal point of the whole cosmos was Mrs. Rieff's finger, tightening on the trigger.

He said, stupidly, "Teddy killed the girl. He was going to kill me. I had to. . ."

"I know. I sent him to do both.' Danny backed off a step. She followed, Death in a nightgown and a flannel wrapper, with curlers in its hair. She said softly, "I want to kill you. I want to kill myself, for killing my son. And even if I didn't, do you think I could let you leave this house alive after all you learned this night?"

"They'll get you for killing me. They'll be here soon."

She laughed, softly. "Look at this room, and you, and—Teddy. Who'll blame me for shooting a crazy killer, already wanted?"

"Frieda. Millie. They'll tell . . ."

"I'll take care of Frieda and Millie." The automatic came up, steadied, rocklike in her thick hand.

Danny said, "Wait. Did you know Teddy was blackmailing Cicely and keeping the money? Your money?"

Her hard pebble eyes blinked. "You're lying."

"Why do you think she was demanding more and more money? Just yesterday, so that you and Halstead both wanted to kill her on the same night. Look in Teddy's pockets. You'll find the bills I stole from the body, and a note."

"You're a fool. Teddy wouldn't have left money on her body, even if he had been lying to me."

"I frightened him away, running across that stone bridge."

Her eyes were ugly with pain and hate. She was only listening with the top of her mind, watching him, thinking how he was going to die.

"What stone bridge?"

"In the La Brea Pits, where he killed her."

"You're crazy," said Mrs. Rieff dreamily. "He drove her car off the road into Coldwater Canyon."

The round black eye of the automatic was staring at Danny's heart.

He dropped, twisting sideways back of a chair. The bullet sang just over his head and thunked into the plaster wall. He cried out:

"I tell you he killed her in the Pits! He jammed her throat down into the mouth of that sabre-tooth cat. For God's sake, look!"

PERHAPS missing her shot had shaken her a little, or perhaps the truth was naked in Danny's voice. She bent, slowly, never taking her eyes from the chair where the boy crouched, and felt Teddy's pockets.

Danny could see part of her, under the chair. He saw her hand draw the bills out and hold them for a minute, and he listened for a siren, praying. But there was only silence.

Mrs. Rieff whispered, "You did. You lied to me, Teddy. You said you couldn't get anything on her to make her stop. That's why we had to kill her."

Then her hand dropped the bills and lay for a moment tenderly on Teddy's face. "It doesn't matter now."

She got up. "It doesn't matter now, does it, you there behind the chair? They're both dead now, and it doesn't matter!"

Danny, under the chair, watched her thick white ankles come slowly toward him. Beyond them was Frieda, lying still, the golden arrow glittering softly as she breathed.

Frieda knew what Teddy had on Cicely. She could tell the whole story of Teddy's double-cross. But she was out. And it didn't matter, anyway. They were both dead, and he was going to be.

The ankles stopped beyond the chair. He could see the veins on them, blue and bunchy. His long jaw stiffened. If he got up suddenly, and pushed the chair over into her . . .

Frieda stirred, just the faintest contraction of the muscles, and the golden arrow shot a wicked barb of light into his eyes.

Danny's muscles tightened. There were fragments of glass and china on the floor from the table he and Teddy had knocked over. He got a handful, caught a deep breath, and surged up.

The chair crashed over, almost into Mrs. Rieff's knees, so that she had to move back. And the handful of fragments shot out like shrapnel from Danny's hand.

They struck Frieda Rieff full in the face and neck. She cried out and sprang up, startled and furious, her face twisted into a devil's mask frighteningly like Teddy's.

Danny shouted, "Don't shoot. I didn't kill your son. She did!"

FOR a long moment there was silence. Then Frieda began to cry softly, the look on her face gone so swiftly that it might have been imagination. Mrs. Rieff said, almost soundlessly:

"What are you trying to do?"

"Save my neck," said Danny. She had her balance again. She could shoot, any time. Frieda was standing with her face in her hands, her wheat-gold hair falling over them, shaking a little.

Danny said, "Frieda was faking. She was waiting for you to kill me. That way I'd take the blame for both murders."

"That's not true." Frieda's voice was a broken, childish sob. "I did faint. When I came to I was scared. I just lay there. How can you say I killed my own cousin?"

For an instant Danny was shaken. She was so soft, so lovely, so miserable.

Mrs. Rieff saw his hesitation. She said:

"You're stalling."

Faintly, then, there was a siren wailing. Far away, but coming. Sweat needled Danny's face.

Frieda burst out, "How could I have killed Teddy? You were right with me all the time. And there's no mark on him you didn't put there!"

"Frieda," he said quietly, "where does that golden arrow belong?"

Her hand flew to her collar, slid down slowly to her breast. "No place in particular. Anywhere. Anywhere I want to put it."

Mrs. Rieff said slowly, "It's always on the collar. It was on the collar half an hour ago. Why did you move it?"

"I don't know. What difference does it make. Why do you want to treat me this way?"

She crumpled into a chair, crying. Mrs. Rieff was staring at her with hard pebble eyes. Danny took a chance. He walked over to her and pulled her head back by the wheat-gold hair and said: "When I was standing at the door with my back turned you took the gold arrow off your robe. What did you do with it, Frieda?"

"I—nothing. I didn't know I did it. Aunt Grace!"

Mrs. Rieff stood still, watching. Danny reached down suddenly and unfastened the pin and held it up.

There was blood, just a tiny smear of it, in the joint of the pin. A brass pin, five inches long, and sharp at the tip.

SHE sat there, quite still, her face hardening like soft clay glazing in the kiln. Danny said slowly:

"You couldn't stab him to the heart with that. You didn't open a vein. But . . ." He knelt suddenly by the body, looking down into the battered, bloodstained face. He found what he was looking for, and felt sick.

"Through the eye," he said. "Into the brain. She thought a little prick like that would never be noticed, in the corner of the eye."

Mrs. Rieff looked down, and then up again, at Frieda. She shrank back, her eyes wide.

"I tell you I didn't! He's lying. Why should I kill Teddy?"

"Because," said Danny, "you killed Cicely, too, and he knew it."

He felt suddenly weary. He didn't even get up from the corpse. He just squatted there, and heard his voice run on.

"You've had bad luck tonight, haven't you, Frieda? You lost your temper and killed Cicely. I saw her body, and I know you lost your temper. Then I scared you away from the money, and you weren't sure I hadn't seen you.

"You saw me. I forgot that. When I turned up here you were scared. Maybe I'd recognize you. I had the money, too, and you wanted that. You felt it in my pocket when you leaned against me out there in the yard, when we found Halstead.

"Only there was Teddy. You wanted to use me against Teddy, and you succeeded. But Teddy got the money first. He knew then that Cicely was dead, that he hadn't killed her, and that left only you.

"Because he knew all about you,

Frieda. He tried to force you to come in with him. Then I knocked him out and tried to keep him for the police, and you knew he'd have to tell the truth in order to save his own neck. So you killed him, with the only weapon you had—that pin.

"You aren't very used to murder, though. You got flustered, between doing it and putting on an act for me, and you got the pin back in the wrong place. You'd have been all right, if it hadn't been for that. But I saw it was wrong, and I wondered why, and all of a sudden a lot of things lined right up and made sense."

Mrs. Rieff said, "You don't make sense, kid." But she wasn't going to shoot. She was looking at the gold arrow.

"I didn't," said Danny wearily. "I'm a hell of a detective. I was fooled, like everybody else, into thinking Cicely was a hard-boiled blackmailer. I went on from there and built up a perfect case against Teddy, just like everybody else. I was almost right, too.

"But I was an awful dope. I swallowed that picture of Cicely you all had, and didn't pay any attention to the Cicely that Millie knew. A gentle, kindly girl who was scared out of her wits and knew something was going to happen to her.

"Would a hard-boiled criminal show all that to a servant? Wouldn't she do something about it? She'd apparently done enough before. And what could Teddy have on her, to make her pay blackmail?

"I didn't think much about that, either. I guess I thought he was threatening to expose her to the police. But he couldn't have done that. He was in too deep himself. So it had to be something else—someone else that Cicely was afraid of.

"I'd never have guessed who, if Frieda hadn't been forced to kill Teddy."

MRS. RIEFF still hadn't moved, but her hard little eyes were intent. Frieda hid her face in her hands. Her voice came small and soft and piteous:

"You're mad! Cicely's always dominated me. I don't know what was between her and Teddy, but I didn't kill her! I wouldn't have the strength. And you said yourself the killer was a man."

"I thought so. I'm used to thinking of pants as masculine. But—Cicely was awfully small, and you're no weakling, Frieda. What did you do with your dark slack suit, Frieda, and the thing that goes around your head and covers up that blond hair?"

She didn't answer, and Mrs. Rieff said, "Yes. Where is it?"

"I gave it away. Yesterday. The War Relief people."

"The police," said Danny, "can trace it, then. Especially with all that blood on it."

"ALL right!" Frieda was standing suddenly, her face white and hard, her eyes startingly like Teddy's, narrow and cat-like. "I changed my clothes in my car. I wrapped the slack suit around a big rock and threw it in the sump of an abandoned oil well.

"Sure, I killed her. I didn't mean to.

I've used Cicely since we were kids, making her do my dirty work and take the blame. She was useful to me. But she went soft tonight. She said she was going to the police, that she couldn't go on this way. I lost my temper . . .

"I was mad anyway. I found out about Teddy. He made love to her while I was gone, and the fool fell for it. He found out all about me, and used Cicely's fear of me to blackmail her. Pretty little set-up, wasn't it, Aunt Grace? Me behind Cicely, Cicely blackmailing you and Halstead and a couple of others, and Teddy milking the lot of us.

"Cicely couldn't keep it up. There just wasn't enough money for both Teddy and me. She had to confess. And by that time, Teddy was dangerous to me. And the rest—well, you're pretty clever, kid."

She turned on her aunt. There wasn't any fear or softness in her. Just tough flexible realism, seeing, weighing, acting.

"What do we do now, Aunt Grace? If you go ahead and shoot the boy, we're both in the clear on those murders. If you shoot me, the police will get you. If you don't shoot either of us, I'll spill all I know about Rieff Blackmail, Incorporated, before I die."

"But if I shoot both of you," said Mrs. Rieff gently, "the boy will be saddled with three murders, and I'll be clear."

Danny hurled himself just as the silenced gun plopped softly. The bullet snarled past his ear, biting a little chunk of flesh from the cartilage. Then he had smashed into Mrs. Rieff.

She was too heavy to move fast enough. The gun spoke once more, harmlessly. Then Danny's fingers had crushed it out of her hand.

He sat down, then, holding the gun on two women who looked more like trapped wolves than women. The si-rens screamed up outside the house, and stopped, and presently there were feet tramping through the house.

Big, heavy feet. And for the first time, Danny Thayer was glad to hear them.

THE END

THE BEST MOTIVE

By Richard S. Prather

There was this lunatic, the girl told Shell Scott, who was going to kill
her. It wasn't the cheeriest subject to be discussing in a haunted night club.

THE cab dropped me off on the outskirts of Silver Beach and I looked around before I walked through darkness down the narrow alley. I didn't see anybody who looked like Bruno, the guy Ellen had told me was due for a stretch at the cackle factory. Any guy who'd try twice to kill a sex-charged hunk of dreamy tomato like Ellen *had* to be one step removed from the net. The crazy guy was probably still around here somewhere; he had been when Ellen phoned me, fright twisting the words in her throat.

I was eighty miles from the Los Angeles office of "Sheldon Scott, Investigations," and I didn't think Bruno had ever seen me. But I'm damned easy to describe: six-two, short-cropped hair, almost white, the same color as my goofy eyebrows, and the face you might expect on an ex-Marine. I didn't see anybody eyeballing me, so I walked to the alley entrance of The Haunt, a gruesome Silver Beach nightclub with lively corpses and a hot orchestra.

Knowing that Ellen was inside made my throat dryer, my pulse faster. She had a shape like a mating pretzel, and the normal expression in her dark eyes always made me think

she was about to tell a pleasantly dirty story. I walked past the grinning Death's head and a luminous skeleton and on into the club, banged against a table and spilled somebody's drink, barked my shin on a chair and got a perfect barrage of highly uncomplimentary language. Man, it was dark.

When my eyes were used to the gloom I saw dark blurs, presumably people drinking or feeling or whispering in ears, or Christ knows what all. Anything could have been happening in some of those corners, absolutely anything. Strike a match and you're dead. The orchestra was just beginning a number. I expected a funeral march or "I'll Be Glad When You're Dead, You Rascal, You," but it was the bright and bouncy "Love Me."

It was bright and bouncy like Ellen. I'd known the gal only a week, but she was already under my skin. And I felt sorry for her, though it's hard to be sorry for a twenty-three-year-old beauty with a million bucks. But she'd had it tough otherwise: both parents killed when she was nineteen, and the man she loved, her husband Ron, had been killed in a train wreck six months ago.

I found her at one of the small tables on the edge of the dance floor. I took a chance and lit a cigarette, and it was Ellen, strikingly lovely, the warm light melting on her high cheekbones, caressing her red, parted lips, and showing me fright in her dark eyes before the match went out.

"Oh, Shell," she said. "Shell, I'm glad you're here." Her hand slid across the table and found mine, held it. My spine wiggled to "Love Me." "This is a *horrid* place," she added. "Ghastly. I'm half out of my wits."

This wasn't the cheeriest spot for a gal who expected to have her throat cut by a crazy man. I squeezed her hand, thinking that no matter how dark it was, this had better be the extent of my squeezing. Ellen Benson was a Reno, Nevada gal vacationing at California's Laguna Beach a few miles from here—with Joe Benson. Uh-huh, honeymooning with the new husband. What the hell; I squeezed Mrs. Joe Benson's hand some more.

"The Haunt," I said. "Our motto is 'We scare you to death.' O.K., honey. What's with Bruno?"

Bruno was the crux. Apparently the nut had tried to murder her twice. She and hubby Joe had seen Bruno get off the bus in Laguna Beach yesterday afternoon; last night the trouble had started. She'd been visiting friends in San Clemente; driving back to Laguna, the brakes on her big Caddie went out, but luckily she wasn't hurt. Then, walking from the car to a service station nearby, where she could phone, she'd been shot at. She'd screamed, run to the station, been lucky once more. Tonight, just half an hour ago, she'd seen Bruno again and phoned me. Because she could reach it easily, and because it was dark enough to hide her—or anybody—I'd told her to meet me here at The Haunt.

She said, "He must have followed me, Shell. Again. It's driving me crazy. Joe and I are going to a party tonight—same friends I visited last night—and we were shopping here for gifts for them. I saw Bruno in front of the shop and told Joe. He told me to get out of sight quick, then went out front to talk to Bruno. I was so terrified I just ran out the back way and phoned you."

I had talked the mess over with both Ellen and hubby Joe last night at the Surf and Sand Hotel in Laguna Beach, where we were all staying. We'd got fairly chummy, and they knew I was from L. A., a private detective vacationing. So when Ellen had got back to the hotel, ready to split at the seams because of the kill attempts, and told Joe what had happened, they'd given me the story. Joe had seemed ready to go to pieces himself. I didn't exactly cotton to the guy, though he seemed nice enough and Ellen had told me he knew everybody in Reno from shoeshine boys to judges, and ex-cons to preachers and they all liked him—probably it's just that I seldom cotton to husbands. A tall, quiet, good-looking man, he'd seemed an odd choice for Ellen. She was hot, sexy, bubbling with life, while Joe impressed me as a guy whose idea of living dangerously was to pick his nose.

I said, "Give me that first Bruno bit again, Ellen."

She said quietly, "After Ron died I was pretty mixed up. This Bruno kept hanging around, but I only went out with him once. He's terribly stupid, and, he's some sort of criminal. I think he was in prison for a while. I couldn't stand him, but I was nice to him—too nice, I guess. When I told him I wouldn't see him any more he went into an awful rage. Said he loved me, he'd follow me everywhere. He did, too. Then just before Joe and I married a month ago, Bruno caught me on the street in Reno. He sliced the dull edge of a knife across my throat and said if he couldn't have me nobody else could either, he'd kill me. He's crazy, insane." Her voice got tighter. "He *kept* following me around. Joe and I didn't tell anyone where we were going on our honeymoon, so I didn't think I'd have to worry about Bruno—and now he's here, he's even come down *here!*"

"Relax, honey, unwind. What say we have a drink?"

We got two highballs as the orchestra began another number and what I call the gook lights came on. The management was putting on its fluorescent act, and in gook light even Marilyn Monroe would look sexless. Ellen's eyes glowed like blue coals. I peeled my lips back and my teeth glowed horribly.

"Oh, my God," she said. "Don't *do* that."

"Sad, huh? You look pretty gruesome yourself."

She smiled and her teeth seemed to leap at me. It was disgusting. "Haven't you been here before?"

"No," she said. "Do people come twice?"

"Sure. It's fun. Look at all the hilarious people."

Dim bodies were wiggling on the dance floor in a whole sea of appalling eyes and teeth that floated in the air. "You ain't seen nothin' yet; pretty quick the skeletons come out." I grinned horribly some more. "But first let's figure what—" I stopped. Somebody was breathing on my neck. In The Haunt you can almost believe it's a ghost's fanny brushing you as it floats by, but this breath was warm, scented with garlic.

I turned around and almost banged into a head angled toward our table. The guy was scrunched over right behind me with his ear practically flapping.

"Hey," I said. "The ear, friend. Do you like the ear? If you do, take it some place else before I remove it."

He jumped back at my first words, his eyes glowing at me. He was alone. I stepped to his table, bent my face down close to his and peered at him. "You get it? Vanish. Get lost."

He didn't say anything. I could see his lips move in an attempt at a smile, but his teeth didn't glow. False teeth wouldn't glow in this light. I sat down with Ellen again and said softly, "This egg looks like nobody I ever saw, what I can see of him. Does Bruno have false teeth?"

"No. Big and crooked, but they aren't false."

"O.K." I looked back at the man

behind me. "The ear, friend. I'll take it." He left, and I asked Ellen, "Any chance Bruno could have followed you here?"

"I . . . don't think so. I don't think he could have seen me go out and down the alley. It was dark."

I kept thinking about that guy at the next table. The loony Bruno would hardly have anybody else teamed up with him. He sounded like an insanely jealous crackpot, and the crack didn't make him less dangerous. Jealousy is one of the best murder motives I've run across, but the crime of passion is usually swift, vicious. I wanted to know more about Bruno—and I was starting to want out of this creepjoint.

"Maybe we'd better take off, Ellen. Anybody wants trouble, I'm all set." After Ellen had phoned and before I'd left Laguna Beach, I'd strapped on my .38 Colt Special.

"Let me finish my drink first, Shell. I'm not scared when you're around. You're . . . good to be with." Her hand tightened on mine, squeezed gently. "Anyway, you'll have to dance with me once. Maybe it'll calm me down some more."

"Ha," I said, "it won't calm me down." I knew what would happen if she laid that long curved body up against me on that dark dance floor. But she was already standing by the table, pulling my hand. I got up.

She sort of oozed into my arms, and into my blood, her free hand restless on the back of my neck. She pressed close against me, following easily, her body soft and warm, even

bold. After about a minute of that I said, "Look. This is lovely, ecstatic, but I, uh, it's too —"

She interrupted. "Shhh. What's the matter?"

"You know damn well what's the matter. What I mean is, hell's bells, after all, you're on your honeymoon —"

"Just a minute." She stopped dancing, put both arms around my neck. "Let me tell you something. Joe wanted me to marry him even before I met Ron, but I just wasn't in love with him. Joe was around all the time, came to the house to see Ron and me while we were married, and after the accident he was wonderful to me, sweet, somebody I could lean on. He was Old Faithful, always there, and good to me—and I thought maybe that was enough. But it wasn't, Shell, and it never will be. A fast honeymoon and a fast divorce, that's it. So there's the sad story of Ellen Benson."

"Joe know how you feel, Ellen?"

"He knows, but he thinks maybe it'll work out. After last night he swore he wouldn't let me out of his sight, and he never did until he went out to see Bruno. He's sweet, Shell; it's just not enough. Now, let's dance."

There was no more conversation until the music ended. We went back to our table and I finished my drink. The gook lighting was still on and I could see two glowing skeletons, or rather waiters dressed in fluorescent skeleton suits with skull hoods, moving around at the far side of the dance floor.

I asked Ellen, "You about ready to

go?"

"One more glug," she said.

I looked out at all the teeth and things again. The two skeletons, looking amazingly lifeless-like, were walking toward our table. Probably something scary was about to happen.

I turned back to Ellen and said, "Glug your glug before we get into the act. Are you afraid of ske—"

It felt like a bony finger poking me in the ribs. For a brief moment light from a pencil flash gleamed on the long-barreled revolver in the man's cloth-covered hand, then flicked over my face and winked out. Ellen gasped, "Shell—"

"Take it easy, honey." I was taking it easy myself. They do some screwy things in The Haunt, but I'd never seen a gun in here before. Maybe it was a gag.

"Look, bony," I said, and that was all I said. I got the gun across my jaw, and a skeleton hand pulled my .38 from its holster, then jerked me out of my seat. The gun jabbed my spine and I was shoved toward the club's entrance.

This was no gag, for sure—and these guys weren't waiters. I stopped, but before I could even think about doing anything, something hard slammed into the back of my skull. I almost went down, and when the guy shoved me I staggered forward. We went out and started down the alley. My head cleared a little as we reached the back of a building, indented a few feet from the alley. The guy shoved me into its darkness. I stumbled and fell to the soft dirt, still confused, wondering what was coming off.

Then I heard a *click* as he cocked the hammer. I was still down on one knee, and as the knowledge that the guy was actually about to plug me jumped in my brain, I acted instinctively, scooping up a handful of soft earth and hurling it toward him, diving to the side and rolling. The gun roared and the bullet dug into earth as I slammed into his legs, grabbed them and yanked. He fell on top of me, and the gun thudded into my arm. Then I was all over him, slicing with the thick edge of my palm, unthinking, just trying to fix him before he fixed me. I felt my hand jar flesh; I saw his face before me and cut at it with all my strength. He went limp. I grabbed him and his head hung like a rag from his neck. I swore, felt for his pulse, jerked off his skull hood, traced my fingers over his split lips, then found the mashed-in bridge of his nose. He was dead.

I didn't know how many other unfriendly guys were back in the club, or what they looked like—but they'd flashed that light in my face and knew me. There was at least one other skeleton there, maybe waiting for this one to return. So two minutes later I walked inside the club wearing the dead man's skeleton suit over my clothes and the Death's mask over my head, peering out of the eye slits. Deep pockets in the black outfit's pants held my .38 and the dead man's gun. Some girls pointed at my glowing skeleton and giggled. I went to the table where Ellen had been. She was gone. The table top was wet where a drink had been spilled.

A voice behind me said softly, "All right?"

I turned. The scent of garlic filled my nostrils. The man smiled, his false teeth dark in his mouth. I nodded, and he seemed satisfied, walked toward the exit. I followed him outside, grabbed the big revolver by its barrel, and when he started to get into a new Buick parked in the alley, I helped him in, with the butt of the gun on the back of his head.

I got into the car with him, and in a minute he groaned, tried to sit up. I grabbed his coat and yanked him to me.

"Talk fast, you son! Where is she?"

He gasped and sputtered. "What . . . what . . ."

I'd yanked the hood off so he could see my face. He looked ready to pass out.

He babbled that he didn't know what I was talking about, so I swatted him alongside the jaw. His false teeth skidded half out of his mouth, and I kept slapping him with the gun until the choppers landed in his lap.

"You've got two seconds," I said. I cocked the gun, and as it clicked he yelped, the words distorted and almost unrecognizable, "All right, O.K. She's—*stop!*"

"Keep it going. All of it. And where is she?"

He fumbled for his teeth. "With Frank Gill. Just picked up her Cad and left. Please, man, watch that gun." He shoved his chipped teeth at his mouth, anxious now, trying to talk even while his teeth clicked in his

shaking hands. "You don't want me, man, it's Bruno Karsh. He phoned Sammy Lighter in Reno last night. Sammy sent three of us for the job."

I broke in. "Where is she? I won't ask you again."

"Other side of Laguna Beach, that bad spot, curve and cliff. He'll knock her out and she's . . . she'll go over in her Cad. Frank's got a Ford out there to come back in."

He kept talking as sickness crawled in my stomach. The next time I laid the gun on him was the last time. I locked him in the Buick's trunk to keep him on ice, then I got behind the wheel and roared out of the alley. I hit seventy going up the winding road beyond Laguna, fear and sickness mingling inside me as I thought of that curve ahead. I knew the place; it was bad enough in the daytime, with a hundred-foot drop off the cliff at the road's edge to the sea below. I shoved the accelerator all the way down, thinking of the Cad tumbling end over end off the cliff, Ellen unconscious behind the steering wheel at the start, and at the end . . . I shivered.

The guy laid out in the trunk had told me more of what had happened, and I knew the Sammy Lighter he said Bruno had phoned last night. Lighter was one of the top racket boys in Nevada. Bruno had wired him money, explained the job was to tail Ellen and her husband, grab her the first time she was alone, and "accidentally" kill her. The men had reached Laguna this A.M., tailed Ellen, and had seen her and Joe spot

Bruno at the Gift Shop in Silver Beach. When she'd ducked out the back way they'd tailed her to The Haunt.

It looked as though Bruno, after a couple of unsuccessful attempts to kill Ellen, had decided to call in the professionals. It also looked as if Joe Benson had been wise not to let his wife out of his sight. But all Bruno had to do was get Joe away from Ellen, knowing the pros would then pick her up, and he'd managed that.

I was peering through the Buick's windshield and suddenly I saw the two cars a quarter mile ahead, above me at the crest of the road. They seemed to be parked, facing in opposite directions, and I saw a man running to the Ford as the blue Cadillac started to roll down the road toward the curve I knew was ahead of it. I lost them for seconds, tires screaming as I slid around the last curve between us, trying not to look to my left at the awesome blackness that was the sea there below me, the wall of earth at the road's right only a blur at the corner of my eye.

As I swung around the last curve the Ford was moving toward me; beyond it the Cad picked up speed as it neared the sharp curve fifty feet ahead of it. I flashed past the Ford, right foot on the brake as I started down the incline, my hands slippery with sweat. The Buick ate up the distance between me and the car Ellen was in, but I didn't think I could possibly reach it before it hurtled over the cliff's rim. The Cad was only yards from the drop when I shoved on the brakes with all my strength, knowing that at this speed I'd never stop in time, fighting the wheel as the Buick swerved, drawing alongside the Cad's left as my headlights fell on the blackness almost in front of me. I yanked the wheel to the right and the jar slammed through my wrists into my shoulders as fenders scraped and crashed, the sound grinding in my ears.

The Caddie swerved and my own tires screamed, sliding closer to the edge on my left as I tried to pull the car around the curve. I saw the Cad angling to the right, pulling away from me now, blackness looming all around me, and then, with the car slowing, I felt the left wheels bite at the road's edge, slide in the dirt, drop suddenly. The car shuddered, hung for a moment, and panic leaped in my brain as I threw my body automatically away from that blackness, clawing for the door handle, jerking at it as the car tilted crazily and moved beneath me. I slammed my feet against the floorboards as the car seemed to jerk and rise above me, and then I half jumped, half fell, through the open door and slammed against the earth, my fingernails ripping and breaking as I clawed at the ground, felt myself sliding backwards, dug with fingers until they bled, then felt the asphalt at my fingertips, pulled myself toward it and sprawled forward on my face.

Behind me I heard pounding from inside the car, hoarse shouts—and suddenly I remembered the man who was in the Buick's trunk. Then the car scraped the cliff's side, crashed with a grating of metal, and there was silence for seconds as it hurtled through the air, followed by a faint splash as it hit the sea. I heard sounds closer to me, looked up. The Cad was a hundred feet away, moving slowly, its side rubbing against the wall of earth at the right edge of the road. I sprinted to it, jerked the brake on.

Ellen lay motionless on the front seat. As I reached for her, light fell on us and I looked back to see the Ford rounding the curve, fast, veering in toward us with brakes squealing. I pushed Ellen to the floorboards, crawled over her and out the door as a gun roared and I saw the Ford stop, its lights off. I grabbed for my .38, yanked it from the deep pocket and dropped on my belly by the rear wheel of the Cad.

Light winked as a man fired and ran toward me; dirt splashed, inches on my left, and the slug ricocheted away whining. Then I was pulling the trigger of my .38, aiming at the man and pulling the trigger again even as he fell and I heard the slugs smack into his body. I jumped up and ran to him, slapped the gun from his hand and bunched his coat in my fist, jerked him up off the ground. I could feel his blood oozing warmly against my fingers. He coughed and a dark stain spread from his lip to chin.

"Where's Bruno?" I realized I was shouting. He shook his head, coughed again. I kept after him and he talked —for a little while. It was the same story I'd got from the other guy. Gill told me the same things about Bruno,

except where he was. Gill also said that after the kill he was to phone the Laguna police and anonymously report the "accident." Then Gill's dead weight hung heavy from my hand and I let him drop to the ground.

It seemed likely that Bruno, perhaps frightened by the mistakes last night, might be fixing himself an iron-clad alibi for tonight's kill. I wondered where Bruno would go if that were true. Probably where there were a lot of people. And right then I remembered some things I hadn't thought about enough; I thought about them. When I finally stood up I was pretty sure I knew where to find Ellen's would-be killer. I left Gill where he was and went back to Ellen.

After what seemed a long time, her eyes fluttered. She started screaming. "Hey, baby," I said, "this is Shell, remember? Hell, I wouldn't hurt a flea." She kept screaming. And she didn't stop until I remembered I still had on that stupid skeleton suit, minus the mask. No wonder she screamed. She thought she was dead and the ghouls had got her.

When we parked in front of the white two-story house with lights blazing inside all the windows, I told Ellen to wait for me away from the car, then I put the Death's mask on, walked to the door in complete costume, and knocked.

A woman opened the door, then stepped back, one hand at her throat. I could hear laughter and music in the room behind her. "What . . ." she gasped. "What in the world . . ."

She backed away from me; I followed her inside the room. People were talking, drinking. Joe looked up, his face shocked and surprised, then flushing with anger as he walked toward me.

Joe Benson, Ellen's new husband. He had stood out like a bright light once I started wondering about him.

As I'd thought earlier, the crime of passion is usually sudden, seldom carefully planned like this one—and the *click* of that skeleton's gun hadn't seemed part of a crazy man's kill. I'd also wondered, finally, how Bruno happened to learn where Ellen was.

Joe shoved me out the door and slammed it behind us. Light fell on his twisted face as he swore at me.

I said softly, "It's all right, she's dead."

In his anger he answered automatically. "But that outfit! And how did you know I was here? None of you knew—" And then he stopped very damned suddenly, his face frightened and ugly, as I pulled off the skeleton hood and he saw my face.

"Now, wait. You don't understand." His voice shook.

"The hell I don't, Benson. I understand a million bucks worth."

His eyes focused on the gun in my hand, and I used it to slam him one between the eyes—and then they stopped focusing.

I dragged him over to the car, shoved him inside, and began to work him over there. At first, I just softened him up, using my fists and not the gun. I didn't give him a chance to cry out; all he could do was moan a little as I kept working on his face. Finally, I took the gun and raked the barrel across his cheek, just once, as hard as I could. That did it. He suddenly starting squirting words. He was really trying to please me now.

"Where's Bruno, Joe?"

"House I rented by phone in his name," he mumbled through puffed lips.

"Where is it?"

He mumbled the address, and I took off my necktie, yanked his hands around in back of him, and bound them together with the necktie. I made the knot as tight as I could, pulling hard until the flesh on his wrists puffed out around the silken tie. Then I locked the car door on his side, shoved him down on the seat, and took off.

It didn't take us long to get to the house, and Joe didn't say a word while we were travelling. He just lay there on the seat, sucking in air through his mouth in huge gulps.

The house was completely dark, and I dragged Joe from the car and shoved him ahead of me up to the front door. I pushed him to one side and tried the knob. It was locked. I turned to Joe and held the barrel of my gun under his nose.

"The key, Joe," I said softly.

"In my coat pocket," he blubbered, getting the words out so fast that he almost stumbled over them.

I held the gun on him, fished the key out of his pocket, and opened the door. I grabbed Joe by the elbow, held him in front of me, and pushed him through the open door ahead of me.

From somewhere in front of us, I heard the muffled sounds of movement, something scraping on the floor. I pulled Joe to a stop and felt along the wall until I found the light switch. I flicked the lights on, and a few feet in front of us was a man sitting on the floor, his hands reaching out for a rope which held his ankles bound together. In back of him were strands of rope that must have come from his wrists.

"Hold it, Bruno," I said, shoving Joe to the floor and pointing the gun at Bruno.

He swivelled his head around and glared at me with eyes that were hate-filled and deadly. Then he caught sight of Joe.

"You dirty son of a bitch!" he screamed. "You tricked me. Where's Ellen?"

Joe just stared at him. I dragged over a chair with my foot, sat down on it, and looked at both of them lying on the floor. I waved the gun back and forth slowly in my hand.

"I think I'll untie him, Joe," I said. "Looks like he wants to get at you."

Joe's eyes rolled toward me and then back to Bruno. "No!" he said quickly. "No!"

"You tipped him off about Ellen, didn't you, Joe," I prompted. "You met him outside the Gift Shop and told him you'd take him to Ellen."

Joe stared at me for a moment, then nodded his head.

"Let's have the rest of it, Joe."

His bloody face twisted up, and then the words began to pour out. "I

had to kill her. Had to make it look like an accident and make sure I was in the clear. Half of Reno knew Bruno had threatened her. I knew if I could get him down here when she died he'd be suspected if anyone was. Sam Lighter in Reno is one of my closest friends; I phoned him yesterday and had him trickle word to Bruno where Ellen was. I figured the fool would come down to pester her if he knew."

His voice trailed off, and he looked at Bruno, staring wild-eyed at him.

"Then you tried to kill Ellen after that, didn't you?" I said.

He pulled his eyes away from Bruno and swung them back to me. "Yes. Lighter let me know when Bruno hopped the L. A. plane, and I checked the bus schedules, made sure Ellen saw him get here. Last night, when she went to San Clemente I said I was sick. I followed her in a rented car. I'd messed with her brakes, but that didn't do it so I took the shot at her."

"So when that didn't work," I said, "you got Lighter to send his boys to get Ellen, lured Bruno here, tied him up, faked the accident, and then tried to have me killed because I would be the only one who knew it was murder, and not an accident."

Joe nodded.

"Bruno was your patsy," I went on. "You had an alibi, Lighter's boys wouldn't talk, and once you had let Bruno go free, the heat would be turned on him. All that was left then was to get me out of the way."

Before Joe could say another word, Bruno let out a wild yell, snaked his hand inside his coat, and pulled out a knife, snapping the blade all in one motion.

"Drop it, Bruno," I yelled at him and started to swing the gun on him.

He never even looked at me. He moved forward, fast for a big guy, and I saw the knife flash upwards.

The knife caught Joe in the throat and stayed there. Bruno started to laugh and rock back and forth on the floor. He was still laughing when I picked up the phone and dialed the police. . . .

* * *

I lay in my bed, alone in the wide bed, in my room at the Surf and Sand, and thought about the mess just ended. Bruno was in the clink; Joe was dead; so were some other guys; and two innocent waiters at The Haunt must still be rubbing their sore heads wondering what happened to their skeleton outfits.

I listened to the whisper of the breakers outside and thought about the Bruno gimmick that had made me concentrate on jealousy, a good substantial motive for murder, and made me wait almost too long to look at the best motive—Ellen's million bucks. That's what Joe wanted, and he had to plan her death when he saw their marriage going on the rocks.

I thought, too, about my own motives. I'd wanted to help Ellen for a lot of reasons. She'd been like a frightened kid; she'd had it tough, even if she did have all that dough. And once, at the beginning, she'd hinted at a fabulous fee for me if I could help. But that wasn't all of it. I suppose I had another motive.

The bathroom door opened and soft light outlined Ellen's full, sensual figure, filtered through the dark lace that hugged her lush curves. It was only for a brief moment, but a moment heavy with promise, and then the light snapped out. I heard her moving through the darkness toward me.

Yeah, I guess I did have another motive. Can you think of a better one?

THE END

BRING BACK A CORPSE

By Brett Halliday

Shayne didn't want to take on the job of finding Homer Wilde's vanishing business manager. But Lucy Hamilton was one of the great TV star's adoring fans. So, within fourteen hours,. the redheaded detective found himself winging his way to New York on a Super-Constellation. Assignment — Bring Back a Corpse!

MICHAEL SHAYNE had never seen his secretary look so happily flustered. She sat in her desk chair beyond the low railing, smiling at the telephone mouthpiece. She was saying, "But it's too early. Mr. Shayne never gets in before ten in the morning and I—"

Her head was pulled sharply around at his abrupt entrance. She swallowed hard and stuttered, "Just a moment, please. Mr. Shayne just came in," then cupped her hand over the phone and said in a small, awed voice, "It's Homer *Wilde*, Michael. Take it in your office quick."

Shayne crossed to the railing in two unhurried strides and leaned an elbow on it, grinning indulgently down at Lucy. "You talk to him, Angel. You seemed to be doing all right when I interrupted."

"Please, Michael," she begged. "Don't you understand? It's Homer Wilde himself. He wants to see you."

"For what?" Shayne shook a cigarette from a crumpled pack and stuck it between his lips.

"I don't know. But it must be *awfully* important for him to call you so early. He wants you over at his hotel on the Beach right after his broadcast tonight."

Shayne yawned and put fire to his cigarette and said, "The hell he does. Tell him to hunt up another errand boy."

Lucy Hamilton's brown eyes blazed at Shayne. Gurgling sounds were coming from the phone, and she removed her hand to say in a dulcet tone, "Yes, Mr. Wilde. I'm terribly sorry, but Mr. Shayne is tied up just for the moment. I'll have him call you right back, if you'll give me your number."

She listened to more gurgling sounds, biting her lower lip anxiously. "I see," she said. "Of course. Just one second."

Again she covered the mouthpiece and turned her head to glare up at her red-headed employer. "He doesn't want you to call him. He just wants you to get over there before midnight."

Smoke wreathed from Shayne's nostrils and the irritating grin remained on his rugged face. "Tell him to go jump in the ocean," he said pleasantly.

"Michael, if you don't . . ." Lucy gritted her teeth and turned back, uncovered the phone to say, "Yes, Mr. Wilde. Mr. Shayne will be delighted. Suite Six forty-two? He'll be there." She slammed the instrument down and stood up to confront Shayne defiantly.

"Mike, I'll never, *never* forgive you if you don't even go over to see what Mr. Wilde wants. Maybe . . . I could even meet him in person, if he retains you."

Shayne's grin faded slowly, to be replaced by a baffled expression. "I never knew you were like that, Lucy. My God! Wilde is nothing but—"

"Nothing but the most important and best-loved television personality in the country," she interrupted, bitingly. "That's all he is. Every girl I know would gladly give her right arm to meet him. That's all!"

Shayne said, "I'll be tripledamned." He clawed strong fingers through his coarse red hair, shaking his head in perplexity. "I never thought—"

"You just never think, period!" she interrupted again, more violently. "Well, I'm a female human being even if you don't realize it, Michael Shayne. If you don't go over to the White Sapphire Hotel tonight I'll never speak to you again in my life."

Shayne grinned again, this time with real mirth. He straightened his tall frame and leaned over the railing to crook his forefinger beneath Lucy's firm chin.

"The White Sapphire it is, angel. Shall I bring you his autograph?"

"You can tell him I'm one of his greatest fans and am dying to meet him," she responded promptly. "I do hope it'll be a long assignment."

Shayne shrugged and said, "Relax, Lucy. I'll go. Now, let's forget about Homer Wilde and get to work." But strangely enough, as the day went on, the detective found it difficult to keep Wilde out of his thoughts. He had never seen the television performer because he didn't even own a set, but he knew who Homer Wilde was, of course.

No one who read a newspaper could fail to know something about him—especially in Miami, where the star broadcast his nationwide shows several times during each winter season.

But he didn't know what to expect when he entered the Miami Beach hotel suite at five minutes past midnight, though it certainly wasn't what he found on the other side of the door—a short, slender, curly-haired man with an engaging awkwardness of gesture and a face whose normal night club pallor was masked by a blistering red sunburn.

He gripped Shayne's hand firmly and lowered long lashes over his eyes with an odd, self-conscious coyness as he exclaimed. "This is simply great of you, Shayne. It's Mike, isn't it? I know all about you, Mike. Read every one of those excellent books your friend

Halliday writes about your cases. Great stuff. Say, now . . ." Stepping back to look up appreciatively at the rangy redhead, "How'd you like to appear as a guest on my show next week in New York, Mike? You'd kill the people. You'd really be a natural. How about it?"

Shayne shook his head and said, "Sorry, fellow. You stick to your last, and I'll stick to mine." His voice hardened. "That isn't why you got me over here, is it?"

"As a matter of fact—no. It struck me just now when I got a look at you." Wilde turned and strode up and down the thick carpet, thrusting hands deep into the pockets of his cream-colored slacks.

"I'm in a jam, Mike. My business manager is missing. Ben Felton. Been with me for years. Just disappeared into the blue. You got to find him quick."

Shayne shrugged and moved over to a deep chair and sank into it while Wilde continued to stride up and down nervously. "Better try the police. They've got the organization and it won't cost you anything."

"Damn the cost! No, I can't have the police in this, Mike. No publicity, see? If a word of this leaked to wrong people all hell would be on fire. Maybe you've read about this dinosaur deal I'm working on to set up a hotel syndicate here in the Beach. There's been a lot of stuff in the papers . . ." He removed one hand from his pocket and waved it vaguely, as a seal might wave a flipper.

Shayne shook his red head and said, "No. I carefully avoid reading any of that crap they print about TV big-shots. What's a hotel deal got to do with it?"

Wilde stopped in mid-stride with a pained expression on his beet-red face. "You don't read . . . ?" Then he shrugged manfully.

"But I'm sure my secretary can fill me in. She's a terrific fan of yours."

"Is, eh?" Wilde looked deprecatorily pleased. "Perhaps she'd like a personally-autographed picture."

"I'm sure she would," Shayne said wearily. "Look. You were hot about me getting over here tonight. So I'm here. So what's the pitch?"

"You've got to find Ben Felton. This twenty-million-dollar deal is hanging fire until I get his signature on some papers. And it won't hang fire much longer. I think the bastard ran out just to queer the whole pitch. He doesn't like it, see? He argued with me about going into it until I put my foot down and reminded him it was my own goddamned money. Then he disappeared. Find him."

Shayne said mildly, "That's not much to go on. If he's hiding out . . ."

"I don't know whether he is or isn't," Wilde snapped. "Frankly, I'd just as soon you turned up his corpse as not. But I've got to know, so I can get on with the deal one way or another. Cottrell's pressing me hard to finalize the thing."

Shayne sat up a little straighter and his left thumb and forefinger tugged at the lobe of his ear. "Would that be Copey Cottrell?"

"That's right. The big hotel tycoon

from Las Vegas."

'Hotel tycoon' was a new way of describing Copey Cottrell, Shayne thought. In his book, Copey was a vicious racketeer who had victimized Nevada businessmen for too many years, and the thought of him infiltrating Miami Beach, with his pressure and trigger boys and his sleek, streamlined modern racketeering methods, was nauseating to the detective.

"Here's a publicity still of Felton." Wilde held out a glossy print. It showed a lean, lined, weary face beneath straight black hair lashed with grey at the temples. "All my people are good news copy. You can get the rest of the dope on Felton two doors down the hall. We're using this whole half of the floor for office space during my broadcasts here at the Beach. Ask for Pinky Reach." He paused, murmured, "Beach—Reach," and chuckled to himself. "I'd take you down myself, but I've got to get out to Eglin Field early tomorrow A.M."

As if on signal, an inner door opened into the large sitting room and one of Wilde's myriad preoccupations strolled into the room. This one was a willowy brunette, wearing russet slacks and an eyecatching halter of the same color. She undulated languidly close to Homer, regarding the redhead with a speculative, heavy-lidded glance, and said throatily, "I'm sorry, Colonel—I didn't know you had anyone here."

"Colonel?" Shayne echoed in mild surprise. "Reserve?"

Homer Wilde flicked lint from his sleeve with a modesty as nonexistent as the imaginary speck of white on his clothing. "Oh," he said, "the boys up in Washington threw me a bone for entertaining the fellows overseas."

He chuckled again and reached lazily for the girl, drawing her casually into the circle of his arm. "Honey," he said, "you better start watching your step. I just put Mike Shayne on the payroll. Mike, meet Monica Mallon, the purtiest little thrush this side of the Black Hills. You know, they always told me there was gold in them thar mountains."

"Mike Shayne?" The girl's lustrous dark eyes widened. "The famous private detective? Just to check up on me?"

Homer guffawed and squeezed Monica while he winked at Shayne. "Among other things, honey. Don't worry, chick—I've hired Mike to find Ben." And, his mirth falling away, "That reminds me, Mike—hadn't you better get cracking?"

There was, to Shayne, a distinctly unhealthy aura about the whole Wilde setup as he had seen it thus far—a definite sense of wheels within wheels, of things-aren't-what-they-seem. He said bluntly, "I'm not on your payroll yet, Wilde. I don't like the smell of this job."

Homer Wilde's mouth opened. His expression moved swiftly from disbelief, to alarm, to entreaty. For a moment, the redhead feared he was going to burst into tears. "But, Mike," he wailed, "I *need* you! I can give you more of my time as soon as I get my writers gassed up and going on next week's show in New York. Tonight's show really broke my blisters. These Miami broadcasts are always brutal. But if you'll only start looking for Ben Felton now . . ."

He paused, then went on with, "It's this way, Mike. Ben walked out of this hotel yesterday morning and vanished into thin air. He didn't even leave a note, he hasn't called, he hasn't wired—and I've never been out of touch with the guy more than an hour, or two at a time in over ten years. Now, of all times, when I need him more—"

Shayne grinned crookedly. "You really want him found?" he asked. "If you do, the police are your best bet. I'm not your boy."

"But, Mike," said Homer, "five hundred a day, plus expenses, and a bonus if—"

"Just about what you pay your office boys in TV, isn't it?" said the redhead. "You can take your job and shove it!"

As Mike strode to the elevator, a pale, weedy young man passed him, going toward Wilde's suite. Shayne, still amused at memory of Wilde's astonishment, scarcely noticed the young man's stare. He drove back to his apartment in a glow of smug self-satisfaction.

II

UPON SHAYNE'S arrival at his office the next morning, Lucy gave him one look and cried, almost tearfully, *"Mike!* You insulted him—I just know you did. I've seen

that look in your eye before, and —"

"What's it like, Angel?"

"It's mean, and sort of conceited," she said. "If I—"

Mercifully, the telephone rang. Lucy grabbed it and said, "Michael Shayne's office. Just a moment, I'll see." She turned back to Shayne. "It's a Mr. Harry Tyndale calling from New York. He says he—"

"Well, I'll be . . ." Shayne cut her off and took the phone.

"Thank God I caught you!" came the hearty, familiar voice. "Mike, you've got to get up here right away. There's a one-o'clock plane. I'll have you met at La Guardia. I can't talk over the phone, Mike, but it's a real jam—a rough one."

Shayne looked at the clock on the wall. It was ten twenty-eight. He said, "I'll be on the one o'clock, Harry."

Harry Tyndale was one of the nicest guys Shayne had ever met—and one of the richest. A rare combination. The redhead had pulled him out of an attempted shakedown the previous season in Miami and they had become firm friends after it was over. If Harry Tyndale said it was a "real jam," Shayne knew it must be all of that.

Boarding the Super-Constellation two-and-a-half hours later, Shayne took a seat next to the window. Just before they took off, a pale, weedy young man slid into the seat beside him and said, "Mike Shayne, isn't it? I'm Greg Jarvis, part of Homer Wilde's zoo. Didn't I see you leaving his suite last night?"

"Maybe." Shayne was none too

pleased. A private detective, unlike a TV star, is not pleased with a fame that makes his face known to too many people. But it took more than curtness to check Jarvis' garrulity.

"I'm one of the writers," he gabbled, "and, brother, is that a rugged assignment! Homer is Nero and Simon Legree rolled into one large, economy-sized package."

He launched into an eloquent dissertation on the obnoxious professional character and obscene personal habits of his employer. Shayne listened fitfully, when he wasn't almost dozing, until, without warning, something happened that caused him to forget Homer Wilde and his companion's complaints alike.

A jet-plane came blasting out of a cloudbank, directly in front of them, less than a mile ahead. Shayne barely heard Jarvis stop in mid-sentence to utter a terrified, *"Jesus Christ!"*

With the planes approaching one another at a rate exceeding the speed of sound, there were but fractions of a second in which to prepare for the deadly collision that seemed inescapable. But somehow, in those fractions of splintered time, the jet slid downward, out of sight beneath them, and was gone.

Shayne slowly unclenched his fists and looked down at the red lines his nails had cut into his palms in so brief and deadly a moment. He again became conscious of Jarvis' voice in his left ear.

" . . . people wonder why we have trouble putting together sensible material for TV. Well, that stupid jet's

the answer—just like this air-wagon we're riding in. The unities have been kicked all to hell and gone."

"What unities?" asked Shayne, wondering if Jarvis really had the faintest idea of how closely death had brushed them by.

"It goes back to the Greeks," said Jarvis condescendingly. "The Ancient Greeks, you know. They devised the unities and made them work better than any dramatic formula since. The gist of them was that nothing could happen onstage that could not happen in real life in the same space or the same length of time that the play took. You see what I'm getting at?"

"And now they're kicked all to hell and gone?" Shayne asked idly.

"You saw that jet-plane, didn't you? Beyond the speed of sound! Time and space are telescoped like an accordion. Anything can happen anywhere, in any time," the writer complained and paused to brood on the injustices of science toward art.

At La Guardia, Shayne bade him a brusque farewell as he was greeted by a liveried chauffeur. The redhead was frankly glad to have seen the last of Homer Wilde's "zoo." He was whisked into the city and up to an immense suite on the top floor of the Wallston Plaza Towers, where he was met by Harry Tyndale in the huge master bedroom.

"Thank God you're here, Mike!" Tyndale was burly and grizzled, a deep-voiced bear of a man. At the moment, his heavy features showed unaccustomed lines of weariness and strain, and his voice throbbed with emotion and relief.

Shayne looked around the room and asked lightly, "What's up, Harry—corpse under the bed?"

"Not quite, Mike," Tyndale took him by the elbow and led him across the room to open a door leading into a bathroom—a silver-and-marble bathroom with a sunken tub big enough to float an outboard motor-boat. Only there wasn't a boat in the bathtub . . .

Instead, Shayne stood staring down at the fully-clothed body of a dead man. A small man, stretched out neatly in the tub with his left temple smashed. There was a livid bruise on his jaw, and a smear of blood on one of the silver fittings indicated that he might have been slugged on the chin and accidentally suffered the fatal wound in falling.

But what interested Shayne most at the moment was the dead man's face. It was lined, wellworn by life, and his dead eyes stared up at the detective as though saying mockingly, "So you finally found me, eh? Even after turning down the job of looking for me."

Shayne had found him. The dead man was Ben Felton, mysteriously missing from Miami.

Shayne straightened and backed out of the bathroom. Tyndale met him outside the doorway with a goblet half-full of Napoleon cognac.

Shayne drank half of it and demanded harshly, "How did he get there?"

Tyndale opened his manicured, muscular hands. "That's the hell of it!"

he said. "I don't know."

"Come off it, Harry," Shayne told him. "You got me here. You know me. Now *talk!*" The last two words were a whiplash.

Harry Tyndale's face reddened—he was not a man accustomed to taking orders from anyone. He said, "God-dam it, Mike, *I don't know!* I've sunk a small mint in a new color photo-printing process that will revolution-ize the field, but I've got other busi-nesses to feed, and my hotels are in trouble. I need every bit of good will and publicity I can get. My public rela-tions counsel said, 'Toss a party . . . a big one.'

"So I did. Last night. I opened up the whole suite and had a hell of a mob milling around all night. In the middle of the morning I came in here and flopped on the bed and passed out. Never did such a thing before in my life. I have a good head for liquor. I woke with a lousy headache . . . just as if I'd had a Mickey Finn . . . and there he was. Some of the guests were still in the other rooms tanking up. I haven't dared leave here after finding him. I phoned you, and I've been sweating it out every since."

"What do you expect me to do, Harry?" Shayne asked quietly. He was convinced Harry Tyndale was telling the truth.

"I don't know," said Tyndale wea-rily, leaning against the foot of one of the twin beds. "If this gets out, and there's a big smell, it will ruin me. I'm way overextended until this photo thing is launched. But get me out of this, and you can name your own ticket."

"You should have called the cops and leveled," the redhead told him somberly. "Now you're in trouble anyway."

"I'm not a complete idiot!" Tyndale's nerves, close to the snapping point, caused him briefly to lose self-control. "Don't you think I know that? But I didn't dare. I thought, that is, I hoped..."

"You hoped a character named Shayne, who got a broad off your neck in Miami last winter, could get a corpse out of your bathtub today," growled the detective. "Dammit, Harry, I wouldn't even try to do a thing like this on my own home grounds. And here in New York..." He paused to tug at the lobe of his left ear. "Tell me something, Harry. Have there been any TV personalities here? Actors, actresses, anybody like that?"

"Not that I know of—*I* didn't invite any," said Tyndale, puzzled. "This was a business party. There are women, sure—what's a party without 'em? You know the type—advertising girls, models, maybe an actress or two. This is a big wingding. But I wouldn't know a TV personality if I saw one—unless it was a newscaster or sports commentator. They're all I ever look at on TV."

He was interrupted by the opening of the door that led to the rest of the suite. Sounds of music and laughter entered, as did a beautifully stacked blonde in a green suit that matched her eyes, a blonde who managed to be attractive even though she was obviously a bit unsteady on her feet.

"Hi, yuall," she said in honeyed accents as Southern as fried chicken and hush-puppies.

"What do *you* want?" Tyndale snapped at her.

"Shugah, ah'm jus' not sure." Her green eyes ranged from Tyndale's defiant bulk to the long lean, muscular detective. "It jus' *cood* be, ah wan' somethin' lak him." She pointed a vermillion-tipped forefinger directly at Shayne.

"Later, honey, I'll buy you a dozen like him," said Tyndale. Moving into action, he propelled her gallantly but firmly outside and closed the door behind her. Turning to the redhead, he mopped a suddenly streaming brow and said, "That's about the sixth time she's come barging in here since I found that—*thing*. You see why I don't dare leave the room."

Shayne suppressed a grin. But the girl bothered him almost as much as Ben Felton's corpse, lying in the bathtub just beyond a thin wood door. Whatever Ben Felton had been, he was no longer. Whatever harm his body could do would be involuntary as far as he was concerned. But this greeneyed blonde—Shayne felt certain, from the wariness of her glance, that she had been sober. He doubted she was a genuine blonde. He was sure she was not a true Southerner. No Southerner ever said *cood* for *could*.

"Anybody else been in here today?" he asked.

"A few strays—but none as often as that one. What a *mess!*"

"How come your hotels are in

trouble while you're all tied up launching this new gizmo? I thought you, of all people, knew how to protect your rear."

"I thought so, too," said the millionaire wretchedly. "It wouldn't have happened if a bunch of gang-backed sharks from Las Vegas hadn't picked this moment to move in on me. When operations get as large as mine, there are bound to be leaks. You can't count on one hundred percent loyalty—not from humans, anyway. The sharks have been giving me the full treatment, all the way from stock raids to bedbugs."

"Who's behind it?" Shayne asked warily.

"Ever hear of a smooth-talking, good-looking, dirty-minded, snake-moraled, twenty-nine karat rat name Copey Cottrell?" Tyndale asked. "He's a no-good, underworld bastard, one of the Buggsy Siegal kind who can curl a pinkie around a teacup with an archduchess and beat up a hold-out whore on his string with a baseball bat half an hour later. Maybe you didn't know this, Mike, but I picked up the White Sapphire, in Miami Beach, three months ago. Seems, by their lights, I made a mistake. Seems they'd set their sights on it. So . . ." Again he spread his arms.

Shayne nodded. "I had no idea you were in the White Sapphire mess," he said. He was beginning to see why Ben Felton should have turned up in Harry Tyndale's Suite. "Harry, if I were you, I'd go hunting for that leak with a monkey wrench."

"Don't worry," said Tyndale. "I'm working on that. And don't worry about my handling Copey Cottrell and all his nasty little men—I've been in dirty fights before. What worries me is that . . ." He nodded again toward the bathroom door.

"It damned well ought to worry you," said Shayne. "It worries the hell out of *me* and *I* had nothing to do with it."

"You never saw the guy before, did you?" It was a forlorn-hope question.

"Nope," replied the redhead truthfully. He paused to glance at his watch as the last pieces of a hare-brained, impossible plan fell together. "Have somebody get a small trunk—one of those steel foot-lockers they use in the army, with a grip on it. Have him get it here quick. I've got to be on the dinner plane for Miami tonight."

Harry Tyndale looked as if he couldn't quite believe it. His deep voice was a whisper as he asked, "Mike, what are you going to do?"

"Harry," the detective told him, "the less you know about it, the better. If I pull it off, you'll be getting my bill—a whopper. If I don't, it will cost you a lot more in lawyer's fees. Now, get going, or we're both up the creek without a paddle between us."

Harry got going. The trunk was ordered, the reservations made, the chauffeur called for before Shayne had time to finish another drink. Shayne sipped it, rather than gulped it, wondering if he had gone out of his mind. He was used to taking long chances, to calculated risks. He was used to getting away with them. But to fly Ben Felton's corpse back to Miami in a foot-locker and dump him in Homer Wilde's lap . . .

He could still hear the television star's musical voice saying, "I'd just as soon you'd turn up his corpse as not."

If the redhead pulled it off, Homer was going to get his corpse.

When the locker arrived, Harry Tyndale locked the room doors. Then, for twelve minutes, he and Shayne were grimly busy. By the time they were through and had washed their hands, the redhead had acquired a sympathy for trunk murderers he had never thought would be his. If the deceased had not been such a small man . . . Shayne poured himself a drink, told Tyndale to have his men take the trunk down to the waiting car, then poured a half-tumbler for a newly grey-faced Tyndale.

"Okay, Harry, now take a reef in yourself and hope for the best."

"Thanks, Mike." Tyndale's handclasp was fervent.

"It's not over yet," the redhead told him. "Keep your fingers crossed."

III

SHAYNE MADE the waiting Super-Constellation with minutes to spare. He had to fork over an extra thirty dollars for overweight luggage and was again grateful that the late Ben Felton had been a small man. To say that he sweated the foot-locker through the weighing-in process was enormous understatement.

If anything went wrong—and he could think of half-a-hundred possi-bilities without stretching his imagi-nation—it meant curtains for Michael Shayne, to say nothing of Harry Tyndale. But once Harry had called Shayne instead of the New York police, there was little else either of them *could* do.

Even if he got his strange cargo to Miami intact, there remained the little matter of arranging to plant it where it could do the most good for the team of Tyndale and Shayne—and the most damage to Copey Cottrell and his gangsters.

Why had Felton vanished? Why had he sought to contact Harry Tyndale? Had he been killed to prevent that contact? On the surface, the answers to all three questions lay in exactly two words—Copey Cottrell. Shayne had heard people call Cottrell good-looking. The detective found his eyes on his own right hand, which had, without conscious direction, balled itself into a fist. Perhaps, if Cottrell weren't so pretty . . .

For the first time, the detective allowed himself to ponder the identity of Ben Felton's killer. At a jamboree like the one Harry Tyndale was throwing, it could have been almost anyone. But for once, the identity of a murderer was not of supreme importance in a murder case. It was what was done with the corpse that mattered to Shayne now.

"Penny foah yuah thoughts," said a rich, feminine Southern voice, almost in his ear.

Shayne's self-possession was not merely a matter of pride—it had been, in hundreds of instances, a matter of life-and-death necessity. The redhead relied on his disciplined ability to withstand the most sudden shocks and never turn a hair. But this time, it took all his self command.

"You again?" He stared coldly at the beautifully stacked greeneyed blonde he had last seen in Harry's bedroom.

"Yaaas, little ol' me," she replied, pouting prettily. "Ah tol' yuah ah jess myught want something like li'l ol' yuah. Ah think it was right ryude of yuah to take off without so much as sayin' gude byah to li'l ol' me."

He grinned in spite of himself, just as the engines of the SuperConstellation cut in, one by one. He said, raising his voice above their roar, "Well, I don't seem to have got away with it—you're here."

There was no more talk until the takeoff. Then she said, "What was that yuah were tryin' to sayah?"

He said, amusement fading as he realized things had gone very wrong, "Cut the accent, honeychil'. You're no more Southern than you were drunk back in Harry Tyndale's hotel room.

"My best friends never told me I could act," she said in a perfectly straight, rather pleasant Midwestern voice.

The damnable part of it, he thought, was that he rather liked this girl—or might have if she weren't such a dangerous unknown. At least, she represented more attractive company than Greg Jarvis, the writer, on the trip up, with his prattle of unities. Shayne took his time studying her, and she returned his gaze, point for point.

She was not quite as pretty as he remembered her—evidently, she was a girl who could project beauty without actually having it. She was also a little older—there were tiny hints of wrinkles around mouth and eyes that told the story. But there was disarming good humor in her not unhandsome face, and then that figure . . .

"Well?" she said. "Satisfied?"

He shook his head. "Far from it . . ." He raised his shaggy red brows a notch.

"Oh . . ." She understood the unspoken question. "My name's Carol Hale, and I'm not married."

He put it to her bluntly. "Carol Hale, why did you follow me aboard this plane from the hotel?"

The good humor became an afterglow, a memory, as she said with quiet determination, "Because, Michael Shayne, I wanted to know what you were doing with poor Ben Felton's body."

Shayne was stopped cold—but not by so much as the flicker of an eyelid did he reveal the fact. He allowed a look of surprise, of bewilderment, to spread over his ruggedly cast features. Perhaps this girl was a poor actor, but the redhead was a good one when he had to be.

He said, "One of us must be crazy."

Mercifully, Carol Hale kept her voice low. She said, "I went to Tyndale's suite with Ben this morning. He went into that master bedroom and told me to wait for him, he had someone to see. I waited—the whole day, and I couldn't find Ben. Then you came in, an hour or so ago, and went in there to talk with Tyndale. You won't deny that, I hope."

Shayne's answer was a shrug—there seemed nothing to say. The girl went on evenly with, "I decided to watch. You see, I knew who you were, though I didn't expect to see you in New York. I used to spend some of my winters in Miami. I wondered why you were there, and I got afraid. Then I decided to keep an eye on the hall. There was another door from the hall to that bedroom. I saw them bring in the trunk. Then I saw them bring it out. A moment later, you followed. I followed you."

Shayne sighed and shook his head. "I'm afraid your imagination has caused you to take a trip for nothing—not that I'm not grateful for a charming, if somewhat zany, companion."

She shook her head, and her green eyes were like twin jewels—hard and cold. She said, "It won't do, Mike Shayne. Tyndale kept watch like a bulldog all morning on that room."

"If you were in there, you must know there wasn't a body there," the redhead told her with an air of patience. "Tyndale was waiting for me on a matter of business. As for the trunk, I'm taking some valuable papers back to Miami for him."

"Mike Shayne playing nursemaid to a bunch of documents!"

"Why couldn't your friend—Ben What's-his-name—simply have ducked out of the bedroom into the hall and gone down in the elevator? He's probably back at the hotel right now, wondering what happened to you."

She shook her head. "Not Ben Felton," she said firmly. "Ben wasn't that kind of a character. He'd have called me—*if* he was able to."

"Maybe he wasn't able to." The redhead was sparring desperately. The girl didn't *know* the corpse was in the foot-locker—but as long as she was with him, she was intensely dangerous. If she blew the whistle on him before he had a chance to reclaim the trunk . . .

"Maybe he wasn't," she said. "He told me the deal he was on could be dangerous—so dangerous he'd been keeping out of sight for seventy-two hours."

"Quite a story," said Shayne, feigning amusement. "And just what was your role in this dangerous deal, Miss Hale? You're not going to tell me your friend brought you along merely as window dressing—not that you wouldn't dress a window damned attractively."

"My role was—or is—very important," she replied serenely. "Incidentally, believe it or not, it was not the sort of part I enjoy playing. But when you set out to destroy a rat, you can't always name your poison."

Shayne shook his head, puzzled. "Somewhere away back there, you lost me. But, now that you're here, what's on the docket?"

Her eyes studied him again. "That," she said, "depends . . ."

It was exasperating. For the time being, there was nothing Shayne could do. He jerked his head toward the window.

"Hell of a beautiful sunset out there," he said.

Carol Hale said, "Isn't it lovely!"

They dined on excellent fried chicken, placed before them on trays by the inevitable trim hostess. They talked—about plane travel, about Miami, about New York, about a score of irrelevant things. But they never returned to the subject of the late Ben Felton, and she never revealed the least thing about herself.

Whatever element she represented in the deadly business, she knew he had the foot-locker aboard the plane and she probably suspected what it contained. If she had actually been with Ben Felton at Tyndale's suite, it was unlikely she was working for what Shayne was beginning to think of as the other side. But he had only her word for all that.

There was no sense in trying to ditch her, once they landed, and walk away from the airport, leaving the trunk to be picked up later. He couldn't risk checking a murdered corpse in a trunk in the airport luggage room, and he felt certain Carol Hale would keep watch and discover any pickup he arranged. A girl who had come along this doggedly on a mere hunch wouldn't give up at that stage of the game.

There was only one thing to do— play out the string, bluff all the way, and keep the girl with him. He shifted his head to look at her covertly. She was lying back in her seat now, eyes closed. She looked harmless and innocent as a—well, baby was not quite the word he had in mind. Quite un-

expectedly, the redhead felt a pang of genuine regret that they had met under such circumstances. Otherwise . . .

The distant barricade of Miami Beach was ablaze with jewel-lights as the big Super-Constellation circled and came in for its landing. A glance at his watch told Shayne they were on time. He stirred, and she yawned dimpling prettily. He said, "Someone meeting you?"

She shook her head, warily.

He added, "I suppose you'll want to stand by while I claim the foot-locker?"

Her answer was, "What else? And if you make one false step, Mike Shayne, I'll call the cops so fast you'll never know what—"

"You will?" Something in his voice checked her.

They were standing, side by side, at the luggage-claiming counter, when Shayne, after a quick glance around said, in a low voice, "Looks as if you won't have to call the cops after all, you double-crossing little . . ."

She said, "What are you. . . ?" And then quick comprehension flashed into her alert green eyes. "It wasn't me," she whispered.

Then, more loudly, "Thanks, Mike, but I can manage by myself. There are plenty of porters here. It was really very kind of you." Deftly, she took the claim-check from his fingers. "Good night, Mike, it's been fun. Hope I see you around."

"Lots of fun," he said grimly. "And more to come. 'Night, Carol."

The redhead tipped his hat and walked away—almost into the arms of an enormous plainclothesman, who was making his way slowly, purposefully, toward them through the small press of porters and passengers and their welcoming friends.

Mike said, "Hello, Len—what are you doing here?"

Len Sturgis, one of the ablest as well as the largest detectives on Chief Will Gentry's Miami Police Force, eyed Shayne distrustfully. "How about you?" he asked. "Why don't you tell your friends when you take a trip to New York? We miss you around here, fellow."

Shayne was in no mood to endure heavy-handed humor. He said, "Two reasons, Len. One, I'm a licensed private detective, and my business is strictly between my clients and me. Two, I don't need to tell you characters what I do—you seem to find it out quick enough anyway. What's on your mind?"

"Nothing special," said Sturgis, looking hurt. "How was the big city, Mike?"

Shayne wanted nothing more at the moment than to get rid of the man. Out of the corner of one eye, he could see Carol Hale sailing serenely toward the cab-stand outside, following a porter who was trundling a pile of bags of various shapes and sizes, among them the brown steel footlocker that contained the mortal remains of Ben Felton.

But Shayne couldn't break away now. He knew Len Sturgis was at the airport in response to a tip, and he knew the detective knew Shayne knew it. Cursing Harry Tyndale and the leak in his inner staff, Shayne tried to think of a way out.

Sturgis prompted him, "No luggage, Mike?"

Shayne took the cue. "Just a one-day trip. I went up on the one o'clock. Friend of mine needed a little help."

Sturgis regarded Shayne with an oh-yeah? look, but said, "Well, I guess there's nothing much doing here. Care for a lift to town?"

"Thanks, Len, but I left my own car in the parking lot outside." Shayne headed for the exit the girl had used.

But he was too late.

She had vanished . . .

IV

IT WAS NEARLY four o'clock the next afternoon when Shayne reached his office. Lucy was in a state. *"Mike!"* she cried. "I've been half out of my mind! You never called me from New York, and I didn't know *what* was going on. Homer Wilde has been going crazy, too. He's been calling up, almost ever since you left. He told me to have you call him the moment you got in."

The redhead grinned as he skimmed his hat toward the rack. "Your idol will have to wait a few minutes longer," he said. His grin faded as he briefed Lucy on the events of the past twenty-four hours. "So there it is." He tugged at his left earlobe. "Somewhere in this city is a woman who calls herself Carol Hale. And with her, unless she's got rid of it already, is a small trunk containing the body of Ben Felton. I've been knocking myself out all day trying to find her. Not a trace, not a clue . . ." He sighed.

There was a glint of wry amuse-, ment in Lucy's brown eyes. "Mike, the damnedest things happen to you!" she said. Then, growing serious, "You say this woman—Carol Hill—was about my height, has a good figure, might be around thirty, with green eyes, and uses an atrocious Southern accent?" Lucy's own soft Southern voice flowed smooth as corn syrup.

"That's about it. Why? Any ideas?" The redhead was pacing the floor.

"And she's a blonde?" Lucy sounded disbelieving.

"She was blonde yesterday," he replied.

"I'd give a dozen pairs of good nylons just to have one good look at her," Lucy said meditatively.

Shayne stopped pacing. "What's on your mind?"

She hesitated briefly. "In the early days, when he was building his popularity, Homer Wilde had a girl in his show called Jeanie Williams. She couldn't sing very well, and she couldn't dance a lick, and, of course, she didn't have to act. She wasn't exactly pretty, but she was nice looking and a marvelous figure.

"I liked her, and so did a lot of people. There used to be gossip about her being Homer's girlfriend. Oh—I remember, he used to kid her about her green eyes. You know, Mike, jealous monster and all that. Then, about three years ago, he dropped her flat."

"Not exactly a novelty where Homer's concerned from what I've been hearing," Shayne told her. "You think my Carol Hale sounds like Homer's Jeanie Williams?"

"Except for the blonde hair," said Lucy. "Listen, Mike, suppose she *has* something on Homer, and suppose Ben Felton went to New York and took her to Harry Tyndale so he could use her evidence, or whatever it is, against Copey Cottrell . . ."

"I'm way ahead of you, Lucy," said Shayne, quietly. "Now all we have to do is find Carol-Jeanie and Ben's body. And after that . . ."

The phone rang. Lucy's brisk, "Michael Shayne's office," cut him short. "Just a moment, I'll see." She looked up at Shayne and whispered, "Homer Wilde, again."

Shayne took the phone grimly and said, "Hello, Wilde, what's on your mind?"

"I've got to see you, Shayne. You can write your own ticket. Any fee you name. Can you come over to the White Sapphire right away?"

"I'll be there." Shayne's eyes were bleak as he put down the phone.

Driving over the Causeway to the Beach, Shayne wondered if Homer had any idea that Ben Felton was dead. Surely he couldn't know that Shayne had found the body, brought it to Miami and lost it again . . .

Wilde was in his hotel bedroom, sitting beside the window looking out at the waters of the bay, silvered by the pre-twilight. The lush Monica Mallon was extended languorously on a chaise longue. She wore dinner pajamas of chartreuse satin, and flaunted a jade cigarette holder. Homer spoke as if she were not there.

"Look, Shayne," he said wearily without rising. "You've got me over a barrel. We're leaving for New York tonight at three A. M. I've got to find Ben before we go, and you're the only man who can do it. He must be somewhere here in Miami. If you find him before we take off, I'll give you a blank check. You can fill in the amount yourself."

"Fair enough." Shayne looked at his watch. "I'll call you before midnight."

"Great!" There was relief in Homer's voice. "And I have a better idea. Come to our farewell party. It starts around midnight in the ballroom here and we leave for the airport at two-thirty A. M. Why don't you bring the charming Miss Hamilton? You say she's a fan of mine, and she certainly has a lovely telephone manner." This with a wink at Shayne, obviously designed to be seen by Monica. There was frost in her glance as Shayne departed.

This time, the redhead stopped at the other suite on the same floor which had been turned into a temporary publicity office.

There, Pinky Reach, the little man with large ears, wrestled with heavy leather-bound pressbooks until Shayne found what he wanted in an old one—a picture of Jeanie Williams. Her hair was brown and clubbed back with a bow. She looked much younger than the body-snatching blonde who had come back from New York with him, but she was un-questionably the same girl.

"Score one for Lucy," he told himself. Then, to Pinky Reach, "This girl—Jeanie Williams—looks like a nice kid."

"The most," was the prompt reply. "Though poor Jeanie's not exactly a kid. She was around when I was breaking in four-five years ago. A sweetheart. We all used to get sore when we thought of her in the hay with his nibs. You know all about that, of course." This with calm assumption that the redhead was up on all such gossip of the show. "Homer *used* her—and I mean used her—for about seven years on his way up. Then he junked her like an old car."

"Wonder what's happened to her since," mused Shayne.

"Who knows?" This with a shrug. "Jeanie dropped from sight. But the story goes that Ben Felton went to the mat with the boss and made him pay off big. That's what started the trouble between them. Homer would have junked Ben, too, if he could, I'm told. Boy, did he boil!" A pause, then, "You picked up anything on Ben? It isn't like him to run out this way.

But Shayne was out of ear-shot by then. In the lobby, Shayne called his office. He told Lucy that she could go home now, and that she was invited to Homer Wilde's party.

He interrupted her cry of, "Oh, Mike. What shall I wear?" to tell her, a little curtly, that he would pick her up some time before midnight, that by then, the case should be solved.

He drove back to his apartment, reasonably well satisfied. Lucy would be pleased at having guessed the identity of his plane companion correctly. And now, at least, Shayne knew whom he was looking for. Everything was neatly tied up except for three large questions. Where was Jeanie-Carol? Where was the body of Ben Felton? Who killed Ben?

He was humming, off-key, a little tune as he went up in the elevator to his apartment. The door was ajar. He paused on the threshold and saw two men sprawled comfortably in two of the easy chairs. They were obviously not the sort of persons to be stopped by a mere locked door.

One of them, a lean, young-old man with a violent sports shirt and a badly broken nose that marred a gutter-handsome face, rose languidly and said, "You Shayne? The boss wants to have a word with you."

"By all means." Shayne matched the mocking courtliness of the intruder. Then, turning to the other, a squat, ugly character with a prematurely bald head, "Are you the boss?"

"Is he kidding?" the squat one asked, getting to his feet. Like his taller companion, he wore a lightweight jacket over a loud, open-collar shirt. The looseness of the jacket's fit did not conceal the pistol he carried in a shoulder-holster from Shayne's trained eyes.

"Shall we go?" said the taller hood politely.

They drove him, in a cream-and-blue convertible, to a palmetto-ringed, ultra-modern house that hugged the ground well beyond the mountain-range of hotels that give Miami Beach its spectacular skyline. Shayne was escorted to a luxurious living room and left there, under the guard of the stockier and stupider of the two hoodlums.

He did not wait long before a compactly built, strong-featured man, who might have been a well-conditioned forty, entered the room. He wore bathing trunks and a brief towelling jacket, and, in spite of the lateness of the hour, there were traces of sand on his chest and stomach. He nodded at Shayne and went to a well-stocked bar.

"Martel, isn't it, Mr. Shayne?" he asked.

"Right," said Shayne, studying Copey Cottrell. The man was coarsely handsome and blandly corrupt. He poured himself a vodka highball and brought Shayne brandy. The two hoodlums had withdrawn to the far end of the long room.

"I've been wanting to meet you," Cottrell said quietly, "ever since Homer tried to put you on his payroll. At first, it didn't seem to me that you could do anything my boys couldn't do. But since yesterday, I've had to upgrade you."

"That's nice," said Shayne, amused by the affectation of urbanity.

"Mind you, Mr. Shayne," went on his host, "I was not in favor of having Felton killed. I deplore violence—it's much too costly a method of doing business. And Felton's death was by way of being an accident. My—associate—in New York lost his temper, which is regrettable—but not as regrettable as the fact that you brought the body back here with you. Ben Felton, found dead in Tyndale's hotel suite in New York is quite a different thing from Ben Felton liable to be found dead at any moment here in Miami. Under certain circumstances, it could be embarrassing. I'm sure you understand."

"Pray elucidate further," said the redhead.

For a moment, he thought Cottrell was going to blow his top. He reddened, all the way from his hair line to the top of his trunks, and his eyes flashed flame. But the flare was brief, and Cottrell did not speak until he had regained self-control. Then he said, in the same quiet tone, "It was my idea, when I was informed last night that you were flying south with the corpse, to have the police take care of it for me. As a taxpayer, I believe in using public servants wherever possible."

He paused, a trifle smugly, then added, "But, in some way you managed to elude the excellent Chief Gentry's detective. This is exceedingly inconvenient. Mr. Shayne, I want that body, and I want it now."

"I'm sorry," said Shayne. "You can't have it."

Cottrell rose from the chair in which he had been sitting while he talked. Jiggling the ice in his glass, he said, "Naturally, I expected that answer. I'm a businessman, and I'm used to making deals. As I told you just now, I sincerely deplore violence. And I'm willing to pay for what I get. Why not? You took some long chances yesterday, but you got away with them. You have something I want. Therefore, I'm willing to pay. And whatever figure we reach will be given you in this room, in cash, once you have given me the information I want. You need not appear in it at all. My boys will take care of the— merchandise.

"What's more"—he paused again, delicately—"the Internal Revenue people won't hear a whisper about the transaction from me. You'll have five thousand dollars and be home free. How does it sound to you, Mr. Shayne?"

"It sounds absurd." Shayne drained his glass. "Even if I wanted to accommodate you, I couldn't."

"Make it ten grand," said Cottrell softly. "Will that do it?"

"I'm afraid not," said Shayne. "You see—I haven't got the body, and *I don't know where it is!*"

"Harry Tyndale would be touched by your loyalty." Cottrell was beginning to turn pink again under his tan. "But I have been told you are a man of such ethics as your profession permits. You've just been hired by Homer Wilde to find Ben Felton. Are you going to fulfill that contract?"

Shayne grinned. "Maybe. But when I found the police waiting for me at the airport, I lost my luggage check. By the time I managed to get Len Sturgis off my back, somebody else must have found it and claimed the trunk."

"Who?"

Shayne shrugged. "I don't know."

"Perhaps we can stir up your brain cells a trifle." Cottrell looked past him and said, "All right, boys. But keep him alive."

Shayne whirled as they came in behind him. The taller hood was swinging a sap lightly, and the half-bald one was drawing a shoulder-holstered gun.

Shayne dropped his shoulder and lunged as he whirled. He caught the squatty one in the belly before he got his gun out, and they went to the floor together.

The gun skidded out of reach, and the man was out cold on the floor. The sap caught Shayne a glancing blow on the side of the head as he came to his feet, and he closed in with the taller man, driving his knee upward into the groin.

The man went down with a thin scream, and Shayne whirled from him just in time to see Cottrell swinging the barrel of a gun viciously. It connected solidly with the base of Shayne's skull, and he went down and out into blackness . . .

V

WHEN SHAYNE returned to consciousness, his head throbbed with pain and the right side of his neck was stiff and sore. It was dark, and his hands were taped securely to his sides. His ankles, too, were tightly taped together.

He was lying on a bed, and there was a window through which he was able to see stars shining above the silhouettes of palmettoes. As memory came back to him, he became aware that he must have been stowed away in a bedroom of Copey Cottrell's mansion. He lay there, waiting for his vision to improve, trying to figure some way out. On the side of the room away from the window, he could see a narrow line of light—a closed door with illumination beyond.

Shayne swung his legs over the edge of the bed and struggled to a sitting position. If it were a bedroom, he reasoned, there must be some sharp angle on which he could work the tape loose that bound his hands to his sides. Until he did that, he was helpless.

He had no way of measuring time, but it seemed to take hours before he finally located the corner of a dresser. It was too high, and he had to go down on his knees and work a drawer loose with his teeth. Then came the seemingly endless, task of working loose broad-banded adhesive tape, professionally applied. He could feel the skin of his right wrist give way before, at last, he managed to loosen the tape sufficiently to get his right hand free.

He was sitting on the floor, freeing his ankles, when he heard the sounds of footsteps approaching from beyond the door, then the remembered voice of the broken-nosed hood, saying, ". . like tangling with a herd of elephants, Louis. My gut will be sore for a week. Better take a look and see if he's croaked or come to. The son of a bitch can't stay out forever."

When he opened the door, inward, Shayne was waiting beside it. As the mobster appeared in the rectangle of light, the redhead moved swiftly, plucking a heavy automatic from the man's shoulder holster before he could raise his arms to prevent the move. The man cried, *"Louis! Look—"*

He had no time to utter another sound. Shayne backhanded him full across the face with the gun and felt flesh and bone tear under the impact. Then he was in the hall, leaping over the falling body and laying the heavy pistol hard against the rocklike skull of the startled Louis. He paused only to strip Louis of his pistol before moving warily, angrily, along the corridor. He walked softly, on the balls of his feet, a gun in either hand, as he made his way out of the mansion. He did not see another living soul.

Outside, the cream-and-blue convertible still waited. The redhead slid behind the wheel, laying his arsenal on the seat beside him. He put the car in gear and got away from there fast. The rage within him was deep. By his watch, it was already past two in the morning, and he felt a sickening sense of time irreparably lost as he burned rubber toward the White Sapphire. He had to find Lucy, and he wanted to be in at the farewell party. There was a chance Lucy might have gone without him, and a possibility Copey Cottrell might be there.

He arrived as the party was breaking up. In one corner, an impromptu quartet was singing *Tamiami Trail* close to a long service bar, which gave evidence of having seen much service. Men and women, looking slightly the worse for wear, were gathered in groups and clusters about the large private ballroom. There was a lot of Air Force brass in evidence.

The little publicity man with the large ears, waylaid him as he moved toward the other end of the room, searching for Lucy. Pinky Reach was a trifle unsteady on his feet and grinning amiably. He said, "You must be a whiz, Shayne. How come you're asking for Jeanie Williams' picture this afternoon? I saw Jeanie in the city this evening."

"Where?" the detective asked sharply.

"In town." The publicity man waved his glass vaguely. "She was with another dame—a real looker. They were coming out of a beauty shop. Antonelli, my assistant, was with me—he can tell you. Hey, Sammy."

Sam Antonelli ambled up and nodded when the publicity man repeated his question. "It was Jeanie, all right," he said solemnly. "Good old Jeanie. Talk about your dames."

"Some other time," said Shayne. "What did the girl with her look like?" He was getting a hunch, and the lobe of his left ear was itching.

"Beautiful!" said Pinky Reach rhapsodically. But, under deft prodding from Shayne, he managed to give a fairly accurate description of Lucy Hamilton. Then he said, mournfully. "Party's almost over. Got to get our bags if we're gonna make Homer's special plane at three."

"That's right," said Antonelli solemnly. "S'long, Shayne."

They wandered away, leaving Shayne frowning. So Lucy had found

Jeanie-Carol—that was one load off his mind. But he'd have given a case of brandy to know where the women were at that moment. His speculations were broken when Homer Wilde came out of another room, surrounded by a coterie of Air Force and other brass, among whom Shayne spotted Cottrell. He lifted a hand in salute and had the pleasure of seeing the underworld boss look briefly distressed at sight of him. "But not as distressed as you're going to look," he told himself grimly.

Homer spotted Shayne and came over to him, hiding his displeasure behind a mask of geniality. "I'd about given you up, Mike," he said. "And where's that pretty secretary of yours?"

Monica Mallon, looking sleek and deadly beautiful in a strapless gown of black sequins, slithered through the crowd and slipped a shapely arm inside Homer's elbow. "Perhaps your adoring little fan isn't quite so adoring as you thought, darling," she told Homer.

Homer ignored her and peered closely at the redhead. "Boy!" he said. "Whatever delayed you must have had claws. You look as if you'd been in a battle royal."

"I was," Shayne snapped. "Ask Cottrell to tell you about it."

Homer, with a look of surprise, glanced at his partner, who shook his head slightly. Taking the cue, Homer raised his voice and said, "Come on! Everybody that's still here, come on out to the airport and see us off. There'll be champagne, and none of

you free loaders will want to miss that." He moved on toward the exit.

Shayne found himself standing beside a trim, young Air Force brigadier, who shook his head and said to the detective, "I never thought I'd hear old Farquar"—indicating an older man with the three stars of a lieutenant general on his shoulder straps—"called a free-loader and smile. Confidentially, sometimes I think Homer's a bit rich for the Air Force's blood. Still, you've got to hand it to a guy who can put on a show the way he did last night and log three thousand miles of jet-flying before a late lunch the next day."

Following Homer, while the brigadier kept on talking, Shayne saw patterns resolve and reshape themselves in his mind's eye. He thought of an Air Force jet blasting out of a cloud bank and all but crashing into a north-bound Constellation as it left Miami—of Jarvis, the writer, complaining that modern scientific development had shattered the unities of the ancient Greek drama. For the first time, what had been mere playwright's patter, took on new meaning.

He said, to the brigadier, "I had an idea Homer's reserve commission was strictly an honorary one."

"That's what we thought," was the reply, "until old Homer decided to make it for real. And once Homer makes up his mind . . ."

Shayne lost the brigadier and got into the back seat of one of a line of rented cars. A man got in beside him and said, "I was hoping you'd show up tonight, Mike. I've been wanting to have a talk with you. What held you up? Wilde told me he was expecting you."

It was Will Gentry, Miami Chief of Police, the redhead's old friend and occasional antagonist. Shayne said, "A character named Cottrell wanted the same answers you do, Will. And I couldn't give them to him because I didn't have them."

"So he held you?" Gentry asked the question lightly, but there was probing below the surface.

"He tried to," Shayne told him.

Gentry said, as they swung for the drive to the airport, "Well, after all, Cottrell's a newcomer around here . . . Those questions Cottrell asked you—think you've got the answers now?"

"Some of them," the redhead replied slowly. "Not all—not yet."

"You know, Mike," Gentry mused, "you disappointed Len Sturgis last night at the airport. We didn't expect you to come in alone."

"I hated to disappoint Len," said Shayne.

"I'm sure you did."

A girl, in the front seat beside the driver, interrupted their colloquy by offering them drinks from a bottle she was carrying. Shayne was grateful for the interruption. It gave him a chance to work out his startling new theory of Ben Felton's death.

The champagne send-off was in full cry when they reached the airport. Shayne got out of the car and moved to the fringe of the celebration, following the revelers through the buildings, out to the ramps, where a big plane waited. He lost Gentry in

the process, but he had not gone far when his sleeve was plucked and Lucy's voice said, "Mike! Thank God you're here!"

Shayne gave her a hug and she put her arms around his neck. He winced as she touched a bruise.

"You're hurt, Michael. What happened?"

"Not bad," he replied. "Couple of other people got hurt a lot worse. I hear you ran down Jeanie."

"She's over there—waiting," Lucy nodded toward a shadowy corner forty feet away.

"Waiting—for what?" asked Shayne.

"For Homer," said Lucy. "Mike, you have no idea of the deal he gave her. Ben Felton protected her for years, but now Ben's dead and . . ."

"I know," said Shayne. "Where's the trunk?"

"That's what she's waiting for," said Lucy. "After what happened to Felton, she's willing to confront Homer and implicate herself just to ruin him. She hates him, but she loves him. And she's really nice. Mike, you've got to do something before she . . ."

"Maybe I can," he said. "How'd you find her, Angel?"

Lucy's eyes glowed in the darkness. "You know that old story about the man who found the lost mule by pretending he was a mule and going where a mule would go? Well, I tried to think what a girl like Jeanie Williams would do if she were planning to confront a man like Homer. The answer was—a beauty parlor. A brown-haired girl would never want to show herself to her old lover as a phoney blonde. So I just went to the beauty parlor show people use in Miami, and there she was. I've been trying everywhere to find you, Mike. How was the party?"

"It was over when I got there," said Mike. "Look out!"

Homer Wilde had seen them. He was moving briskly toward them. Out of the building behind him came a string of porters pushing luggage toward the waiting plane. Homer was effusive to Shayne's secretary.

"You let me down, baby," he complained, holding her hand in both of his. "I had a lot of things planned for you."

"I'll just *bet* you did!" The ever-watchful Monica appeared at Homer's side, breaking up the scene.

Homer laughed at her, and Lucy managed to get her hand free.

"There it is now, Mike!" she whispered, pointing at a load pushed by one of the porters. "She left it in the luggage room at the airport this evening, and got one of her old pals in the show to put it in with Homer's luggage when it got here tonight."

"Now I see what you mean by 'confront'," Shayne whispered in return. "Try to keep her out of this."

"I will, Mike." Lucy slipped away in the shadows.

Homer's eyes were on Shayne. He said, "Well, what about Felton?"

"Your worries," said Mike, "are just about over. Or maybe they're just beginning." He moved toward the plane, calling, "Will—Will Gentry. Something funny here."

He reached the trunk and bent over it, as Will Gentry joined him.

He pointed to a small spot of rust on the foot-locker. "Looks like blood to me, Will. Better open this one up."

Gentry gave Shayne a long, level look. "I'd say it was rust," he said quietly, "But—under the circumstances..." The chief of police gave the order to open the trunk.

LATER, at Police Headquarters, Gentry said, "Hell, Mike, we've got Homer cold—motive, opportunity, even concealing and trying to remove the corpse. Cottrell is caught, too, as a material witness. He'll be bailed out, of course, but he'll have to testify or take a powder. You know how characters like him hate the limelight. Mike, you've done a good night's work."

He paused to fix the detective with a saturnine gaze, added, "Mind you, there are some elements I don't yet understand in this business. But the Air Force has asked me to soft-pedal investigation in certain directions. I'm not even going to ask you how you knew there was a body in that foot-locker, Mike..."

"Thanks, Will," said Shayne, reaching for his hat. "Maybe I'll tell you when you've got Homer put away for keeps."

Lucy and Jeanie Williams were waiting for Shayne at his apartment. Jeanie, much younger with brown hair, stood up with tears in her eyes. "You did a wonderful thing, Mike Shayne, saving me from turning in a man I once loved. It would have exposed my whole sordid story to the tabloids."

He grinned. "I ought to thank you, Jeanie Williams, for snatching that body for me. Did you know Ben Felton was planning to have it out with Homer Wilde in Tyndale's suite yesterday morning?"

She shook her head. "Did Homer plan to kill Ben there?" Her anxiety was evident.

Shayne nodded. "That's why Homer tried to hire me to find Felton the night before he took off in an Air Force jet-plane for Mitchel Field. I was part of his alibi. The Air Force brass thought he was just a reserve officer getting in some flying time when and where he could. Actually, he wanted to stop Ben before Ben got to Harry Tyndale, and he thought that I and the jet-flight together would give him an unbreakable alibi.

"Ben must have told Homer he was taking you to Tyndale's. When you were separated from Ben in the crowd left over from Harry's party, Ben met Homer and Homer took him into Harry's bedroom, knowing Harry would be dead to the world until noon after that drugged drink. Wilde hit Ben and killed him. Then he went back to Mitchel, where his plane had been fueled and flew back to Eglin in time for a late lunch—and damned near hit the plane I was in, leaving Miami on my way to help Harry.

"That writer, Greg Jarvis, was right. Supersonic jet-planes have messed up all the unities, to say nothing of the alibis. It's almost possible for a man to be in two places at once now, and that's going to make life a lot harder for detectives."

Shayne sighed and reached for the brandy.

THE END

"Just a minute, buddy. I'll be right wit' cha!"

ALIBI IN REVERSE

By Robert Leslie Bellem

Nosey Logan had a peach of an alibi; so perfect it was foolproof.
But if he'd been without one, he'd have been safer!

THE MERE act of ringing Pop Conway's doorbell that night made Jarnegan of the homicide division feel like a louse. Ever since Jarnegan's rookie days Pop had been his mentor and friend, helping him over the rough spots, teaching him the job of being a good copper. It was tough to be calling on the old man now on a mission like this one.

Jarnegan thumbed the bell push again, wondering why it took so long to get an answer. Pop was probably puttering around with the sound recording gadgets that had become his hobby in retirement, the homicide dick concluded. Frowning, he rang a third time.

The door opened and Pop Conway blinked out at him, looking a lot older now that he was off the force.

"Tim, my boy! It's good to see you. Come in."

Jarnegan walked into a living room littered with microphones, record players, electrical stuff. His frown deepened. Much of this equipment had belonged to Pop's only son, an expert until his death in an auto accident a few years back. For Pop to be using it now seemed almost morbid, Jarnegan thought.

Pop peered at him.

"Why the scowl, Tim? What's eating you?"

"Nothing much," Jarnegan lied. Plenty was eating him. "Did you hear the news broadcast tonight?"

"No. Anything important on it?"

Jarnegan squared his shoulders.

"Look, Pop. This is screwy, but I've got some questions to ask you."

"Fire away."

"Do you remember a cheap crook named Nosey Logan that used to be mixed up with Ace Cullane's gambling syndicate?"

"Sure I remember," Pop said. "We sent him up for three years on a bunko rap. It was Ace Cullane, the guy he worked for, whose testimony nailed the lid on him. We figured it was another case of thieves falling out—a big one feeding a little one to the wolves."

"Yeh. And remember how Logan threatened to get even with Ace Cullane some day. Yelled it right out in the courtroom."

"Well?"

"Well, Nosey Logan was released from stir this morning. And tonight we found Ace Cullane bumped off in one of his hideaway apartments. A

The expression of alarm in Pop's eyes came too late to warn him . . .

neighbor phoned in the beef, described a guy he saw coming out of Cullane's flat. The description fits Logan so we picked him up on suspicion."

"And—?"

Jarnegan blurted out the words that were festering inside him.

"Logan is trying to use you for an alibi, Pop. He says he was here with you all evening. Ever hear anything so damned crazy?"

"Not crazy, Tim. True."

Jarnegan stared. He felt his neck swelling, making his collar too tight.

"I don't believe it. You wouldn't

have any truck with a wrong guy like Nosey Logan. You wouldn't even let him in your house. Why should you be fronting for the heel?"

Pop Conway smiled softly.

"If anybody but you called me a liar, Tim, he'd get a poke on the horn. I tell you Logan was here at the time of the kill. He was nowhere near the scene of the killing.

"You're sticking to it, then?"

"I'm sticking to it."

Jarnegan sighed.

"Let's go to headquarters. Maybe they'll fall for it. I don't."

Pop was staring past him, looking startled. A warning came to his lips but Jarnegan never heard it. Somebody slugged the homicide detective over the back of the skull with a blackjack. He went down like a chopped tree.

THE ROOM looked like the aftermath of havoc when Tim Jarnegan woke up. Pop Conway wasn't there. Wherever he had gone, though, it had not been willingly. Jarnegan knew this from the evidence of the struggle Pop had made. Furniture was overturned, electrical apparatus scattered, a stack of records smashed. About the only piece of unbroken equipment was a box-like contraption over in a far corner, near the telephone.

Jarnegan made for the phone, his legs unsteady, his head throbbing. Pop had been kidnaped, he realized, but he was too groggy to figure out a possible motive; too dazed to link it with the Ace Cullane kill and Nosey Logan's alibi. All he thought about

was the old man's present danger. Headquarters had to be notified.

He lifted the phone out of its cradle. This caused a subdued hum to issue from the nearby box-like contraption, together with a faint scratchy sound. Restoring the telephone to its prongs stopped these noises.

Puzzled, Jarnegan opened the hinged lid of the box and saw a turntable with a grooved metal record-blank on it. A swivel arm projected over the record, its diaphragm and cutting needle resting in a groove halfway toward the center label. Wires ran down inside the box, vanished there.

The outfit was electrically connected to the telephone in such a way that its machinery functioned only when the circuit was in use. By picking up the phone you started the turntable revolving and your conversation was recorded on the blank metal disc. Jarnegan proved this to his own satisfaction after he got through calling in his report to headquarters. He located the playback pickup, set the needle in its groove, started the mechanism. From a concealed loudspeaker came his own voice repeating what he had just said to the desk sergeant downtown.

Beyond doubt the device was just another ramification of Pop Conway's hobby, a toy to be tinkered with. Now Pop had been snatched, you might say in the very act of supplying an alibi for Nosey Logan. For the first time, Jarnegan began to wonder if the kidnaping had a connection with that alibi.

ON AN idle hunch, he decided to play back the entire record on the turntable to find out what telephone conversations Pop might have had during the day. The first few that came out of the loudspeaker were common place, desultory. Then this mechanical eavesdropper began repeating something that made Jarnegan go tense.

There was Pop's voice to begin with, as if answering somebody's call.

"Hello. Conway speaking."

"Yeah? Well, listen, copper. This is Nosey Logan. Maybe you remember me. I'm just outa stir, see? I was sent up—"

"Yes, Logan," Pop's voice interrupted. "I remember you."

"Okay. Now get this. I'm gunnin' for Ace Cullane, see? He ratted on me three years ago, an' tonight I'm gonna get even. But the law ain't gonna touch me for it afterward on account of you're gonna be my alibi."

Amazement knifed into Pop's reproduced voice.

"Are you crazy?"

"Naw. I said you're gonna alibi me an' I mean it. Unless you'd sooner have me spill the dirt about your son. Sure I know he's dead now. But it wouldn't do his memory no good if I was to tell the way he sold wire-tappin' outfits to the bookie syndicates."

"Wire-tapping?"

"Yeah, gadgets that you could cut in on telegraph trunk lines so the sure thing boys get horse race results

ahead o' time an' clean up on sucker bets."

"My son made and sold outfits like that? To crooks?"

"You heard me. And while you was a cop, too. So how about it? You gonna front for me if I need you, or do I shoot off my yap?"

"I suppose I'll front for you," Pop Conway's voice sounded far-off, weary. "For my son's sake. For the sake of his memory."

"Swell. In case anything comes up, you say I was with you all evenin', see? And don't make no slips." The conversation ended with scratchy silence on the metal record.

JARNEGAN'S HEART was hammering as he stopped the turntable. Now he had the riddle's answer. He knew why Pop had tried to alibi Nosey Logan. The poor old guy had been blackmailed into it, on pain of having his dead son's misdeeds exposed. This discovery led Jarnegan's thoughts into still other channels more closely connected with Pop's kidnaping. He had a hunch about that, too.

Headache forgotten, he sprinted outdoors to his car and aimed it downtown. At Central Precinct he ordered Nosey Logan brought to him from the detention tank to the goldfish room.

Logan swaggered in, a sallow little rat with a certain rodent bravado.

"Hi, shamus. You check my alibi?"

"I checked your alibi," Jarnegan admitted, not mentioning the recorded shakedown conversation whereby Logan had blackmailed Pop

Conway into furnishing it.

"Conway clear me?"

"He said you were with him."

"Then how's about turnin' me loose?"

"Not until I ask you something. Who's your worst enemy now that Ace Cullane has been croaked?"

Logan made a puzzled mouth.

"I don't get you."

"I mean somebody who hates your guts so much he wants you to go to the chair for bumping Cullane."

"But I didn't bump Cullane! I—"

Jarnegan nodded patiently.

"Sure, sure. Pop Conway is your alibi. But he's been snatched."

"What?"

"Yeh. And without Pop's testimony you can't beat the rap. That's obvious. And I think it explains Pop being kidnaped—so he won't be on deck to front for you. Whoever grabbed him is trying to slip you a ticket to the hot squat, Nosey."

"Gawd!"

"So you see why I asked you about your enemies. Who hates you enough to want you fried?"

Logan made gulping sounds in his throat.

"Dice Vallardo—he's the only one! You know him?"

"I know Vallardo. He's been teamed up with Cullane in the rackets quite a while. You think he packs a grudge against you?"

"Damn' right! I crossed him one time. So he got Cullane to go in court an' spill enough to send me up the river. Vallardo did it. He was behind the stretch I got."

Jarnegan nodded.

"It makes sense. And now you think Vallardo heard the news broadcast about you using Pop Conway for an alibi—and he had Pop snatched."

"Yeah. Look. Even if Vallardo knows I didn't croak Cullane, he wants to frame me for it. That keeps him in the clear, see?"

"Are you accusing Vallardo of the kill?" Jarnegan asked.

"Well, he'll take over all the rackets now that Ace is dead. He won't have no partner to share the dough with."

Jarnegan's handcuffs glittered out of his pocket. He snapped them on Logan's wrists.

"Come along. We'll go see Vallardo right now. If he's got Pop Conway, God help him."

The little crook went pasty.

"Ix-nay, copper! I ain't goin' anywheres near Dice Vallardo. Especially with bracelets on. You think I wanna get my kidneys kicked out?"

"I'll kick your kidneys out myself if you don't get moving," Jarnegan said. He yanked his prisoner out to the street and pointed to his car. "In. Fast."

Nosey Logan got in, trembling.

THE PENTHOUSE apartment on the roof of the San Marcal Hotel rented for thirty-five thousand a year. Dice Vallardo paid this out of his small change pocket and had enough left over for gold tipped cigarettes. He was smoking one of the cigarettes in a long ivory holder when Jarnegan marched in with Logan. He put the cigarette down and his hand went surreptitiously toward a desk drawer.

Jarnegan shook his head.

"If you've got a gun in there, better let it alone. Mine's already out." He displayed the snub-nosed .32 special in his fist.

"Have it your way, copper," Vallardo said smoothly. His voice matched his hair, sleek and oily. Sun lamps gave him a healthy tan the year around. He cast a flickering glance at Nosey Logan. "Hello, skunk."

Logan didn't answer. Tim Jarnegan pitched his own tone to a conversation level.

"Where's Pop Conway? I want him. Now."

"What makes you think you'll find him here, copper?"

"A hunch. You snatched him to keep him from giving this Logan louse an alibi."

Vallardo smiled politely.

"You'll have a terrific time proving that, pal."

"I don't need to. I'll just tell you that you haven't any valid reason to hold Pop. He won't alibi Logan, after all."

Nosey Logan let out a yelp and brandished his handcuffs.

"Like hell Pop won't alibi me! You already said—"

"Forget what I said," Jarnegan growled. "You blackmailed him into fronting for you. You phoned him, threatened to expose his dead son's connection with the gambling syndicate's wire-tapping gadget. He was forced to agree to anything you wanted. But he made a record of your telephone conversation and I've lis-

tened to that record. If necessary I'll play it in court—and Pop's testimony will be branded as prejury."

Logan's sob rose to an animal whine.

"But I didn't bump Ace Cullane! I went to his joint, yeah—but he was dead when I got to him. Somebody made the grade ahead of me. It was Vallardo, here! *He* wanted Cullane's rackets—" All of a sudden the manacled little crook sprang at Dice Vallardo.

Jarnegan picked up a chair, hefted it. He yelled:

"Look out, Vallardo! Get him!"

Vallardo opened his desk drawer and came up with an automatic. He fired point blank. He got Nosey Logan through the heart. He looked at Logan's corpse, and then he looked at Jarnegan.

"That finished him copper."

"It finished you, too," Jarnegan said, and hit Vallardo with the chair. It was an extremely heavy chair. This was very tough on Vallardo. He had a soft skull, anyhow.

JARNEGAN walked out of the room and started prowling the rest of the penthouse apartment. He found Pop Conway trussed and gaged in a rear bedroom. He cut the ropes and removed the gag.

"You okay, Pop?"

"Yes. I'm okay. But I—I heard a shot just now, Tim. I—what happened?"

"Vallardo killed Nosey Logan when Nosey accused him of the Cullane croaking. So I guess the accusation was a bull's eye. Anyway, I'll put it down on my report. And Vallardo won't beef. He's dead too. I hit him harder then I thought. Jarnegan made a sour mouth. They're all dead—Cullane, Logan, Vallardo. That closes the case. It just about wipes out the gambling syndicate, too. Which is a good thing."

"But look, Tim," Pop said slowly. "Suppose you're wrong. Suppose Vallardo was innocent of the Cullane kill?"

Jarnegan's eyes held a queer look.

"Then he just got paid off for shooting Nosey Logan, is all. What do you care?"

Pop Conway tried to say something. The words seemed to stick in his throat. "I—I—"

"So all right," Jarnegan said. "So you had a kid you thought the world of. He got messed up with a bunch of crooks, Cullane and Vallardo and their mob. He made wire-tapping gadgets for them. Later he died in an auto accident, only it wasn't an accident. It was deliberate. Cullane and Vallardo had him knocked off, maybe because he had become dangerous to them or wanted to go straight.

"You always suspected his death wasn't an accident but you didn't have any way of proving it so you kept quiet. Then, today, Nosey Logan phoned you and blackmailed you for an alibi he thought he was going to need.

"He talked just enough to make you sure your kid had been murdered by Cullane and Vallardo. You still couldn't prove it in court, so you took the law in your own hands. You went to Cullane's hideout apartment and browned him before Logan could do the job. Then you gave Logan an alibi because it would also be an alibi for yourself. Later, Vallardo had you kidnaped. You permitted this, because you thought it might give you a chance to get Vallardo too. Only I got him first."

Pop looked very old and very tired.

"I made a good cop of you, Tim. You've got it right. All of it. What are you going to do about it?"

"Me?" Jarnegan raised an eyebrow. "Why, hell. A bunch of heels have got their just deserts. I'm not going to do anything about it—except take you home. I told you this case is closed. What chance would I have to prove any of this in court?"

THE END

DETECTIVE MYSTERY MAGAZINE

Writers & Artists Guidelines

Send all fiction submissions as a Word Document (.doc) file attachments via email to fortunapublications@gmail.com.

Fiction:

We are looking for Detective and Mystery fiction. Fiction may range from 1,000 to 40,000+ words. We pay $.001-.01/word on publication for First North American Serial Rights.

Artwork:

Submit samples (jpg) to the email address above. We are seeking detailed, realistic work. We pay $25 for full-page (8.5 x 11 inch) B&W interior illustrations and $75 for full-color cover art.

MURDER AMONG THE DYING

By G. Wayman Jones

Conclusion

CHAPTER VII
Clue of the Scabbard

THE Black Bat reached Carlin's apartment in the Madelon without trouble. He listened outside the door. It was just after midnight and he heard no sound from within.

Opening the door was accomplished with practised deftness and silence. He stepped into an apartment that was lavish to the extreme. A lot of money had gone into furnishing this place, and it was big—at least seven rooms.

The Black Bat investigated each of them, after merely glancing inside to be certain Carlin was not at home. One door resisted his efforts to open it. He had fitted a slim bit of steel into the lock when he noticed that no ordinary burglar tool was going to unlock this particular door.

The lock was modern, expensive, and clevery constructed to resist such attempts. There must have been something in that room which Carlin didn't want anyone to see. But the Black Bat turned away from it to investigate Carlin's rather small study.

From experience the Black Bat knew that a desk, even in a private home can reveal more information than any other piece of furniture, except perhaps a safe. He sat down behind the desk in the little study and started to open drawers. Then his eyes rested upon an ornate scabbard which lay on top of the desk.

He picked it up, reached beneath his coat and drew out the knife which had been used in an attempt to kill Silk. The blade fitted into the scabbard snugly. They were made for one another and the design on the haft of the weapon matched that on the scabbard. The Black Bat withdrew the blade and put it into his pocket again. The scabbard went back on the desk.

He spent about an hour going through Carlin's possessions, something which would have been impossible, without a lot of red tape, if he operated within the law. Carlin, he discovered was not a wealthy man, but his accounts were substantial, and the Black Bat noticed that he had deposited a large sum—twenty-five thousand dollars—in one bank. The money had been in cash, too, according to a duplicate deposit slip inside

the book. Most of the other deposits were above two thousand.

Carlin's clothing was all of the same type. He went in for wide stripes or checks mostly. Other than this, however, the Black Bat found no direct proof that Carlin was behind the attempts of murder. Certainly, though, the knife used on Silk was Carlin's property, and he did answer the description given by the hophead.

The locked door still intrigued the Black Bat. He sat down to wait for Carlin. It had been unnecessary for him to turn on any lights, so he waited patiently in the darkness, eyes closed and brain working over the events of the last couple of days.

He accepted as definite the fact that Victor Shea had written that strange letter and tried to keep the appointment. Shea had been disap-

pointed in not inheriting a considerable estate. His cousin, William B. Wayne, had given a clever motive for young Shea's suicide, but Wayne's hands were not exactly clean. He had inherited the estate and murder had been committed for sums far less than old Joel Shea's fortune.

The chemist, Lyle Alexander, was either an excellent actor or innocent. Yet he had indicated that Victor had burned all his laboratory notes— something highly improbable.

Attorney Buckley sided with Wayne, of course, but Buckley was a smooth, wary opponent. He had been Joel Shea's lawyer also, and would know about any will leaving the property to Wayne.

The animosity between Carlin and Wayne was unusual. Wayne's insults had rolled off Carlin easily, yet they must have been friends once because Carlin seemed to have been an accepted visitor prior to Victor's death.

The only motive, so far taking shape, was that of Wayne's greed for the estate. The chemist, as Silk had suggested, might have a hidden motive concerned with something in the laboratories at the dye plant. If Victor's lab notes had been destroyed after his death, that was good and sufficient reason for suspicion.

But of them all, Carlin offered the best possibilities, except so far as motive was concerned. The Black Bat glanced at his watch. It was after one in the morning now. He had been waiting in the apartment a long time.

Then he heard a key inserted in the door. The Black Bat arose and quietly concealed himself behind drapes that reached to the floor. He had already cut a small slit in the material so that he could witness Carlin's activities if he came into this room.

Carlin carried something wrapped in a crumpled newspaper. He laid the package on the desk. Removing his hat and coat, he smiled smugly and unwrapped the package. The Black Bat barely restrained a cry of surprise and anxiety. Carlin was holding a woman's handbag, and the last time the Black Bat had seen that handbag, it had been under Carol Baldwin's arm.

CARLIN dumped the contents on the desk and started examining everything minutely. He was absorbed in this task when he noticed a weird shadow across the further wall, and at the same instant the cold muzzle of a gun touched the back of his neck.

"Get up!" the Black Bat ordered. "Keep your hands away from your pockets."

A black-clad hand and sleeve flashed by Carlin's face and turned out the desk light, plunging the room into darkness. Then Carlin felt himself being searched.

"What is this?" he demanded. "Who the devil are you? Whatever it is you want, it won't be here!"

"I'm the Black Bat, Mr. Carlin. You have nothing I want except a little information."

"The Black Bat!" Carlin sat down weakly. "I—I don't know why you should be here. I haven't done anything."

"Then what are you afraid of? I've been here for some time, Mr. Carlin. I like your quarters. They are in excellent taste. Even small details are to my satisfaction. Like that scabbard on the desk, for instance. Didn't it come equipped with some kind of a dagger?"

"It's the case for a letter-opener." Carlin wet his lips. "I—lost the knife part. One of the maids who comes in here probably appropriated it. What do you want with me anyhow?"

As he spoke, Carlin slowly stretched one hand across the top of the desk and started to close his fingers around a heavy ash-tray. One blow with this and he would eliminate the danger of the Black Bat. But the edge of a gloved hand struck his wrist a sharp blow, paralyzing the nerves. Carlin gave a bleat of alarm.

"You'll live longer if you don't try any stunts," the Black Bat advised. "Get up and unlock the door to that back room. I'm interested to see what's inside."

"It's just a small photo lab," Carlin grumbled. "You've got your trails twisted somehow. There's no reason why the Black
Bat should come here."

"There is a reason—Victor Shea."

Carlin's eyes went wide in astonishment, and in them was fear. The Black Bat saw this clearly despite the darkness.

Carlin asked permission to reach for his keys, withdrew a leather case and extracted a long, slim key. He preceded the Black Bat to the locked door, opened it, and started to turn on the light.

"Let that switch alone," the Black Bat said sharply. "Well, you did tell the truth. It is a photo lab. What do you do—specialize in photostats? I see a table all set up with equipment for that purpose."

"I experiment with all sorts of pictures." Carlin seemed to be more at ease now. "Look here, if I can help in any way about proving that Victor's death was murder, count on me. I have no evidence, but I'm sure he was killed."

"Just why?" the Black Bat queried. "And who would be a logical suspect?"

"Listen!" Carlin said excitedly. "The old man was sick, yes, but nobody expected him to die so soon. Maybe he was murdered too. And Bill Wayne hated Victor—because all along it was believed that Victor

would inherit the business. Wayne used to be nice to me then because I was Vic's friend. Now he hates me. He's afraid I may find out something. If I did, I'd tell you or Mr. Quinn— he's the Special District Attorney working on the case."

"Just where did you come from tonight?" the Black Bat changed the subject swiftly to ask.

"Why, I was at Wayne's early in the evening. He got me sore and I went to a movie to cool off. Then I had a few drinks at some bar and walked home. I—"

"You're a funny person," the Black Bat interrupted. "One-third of what you tell is the truth, one-third guess work and the last third out-and-out lies. Don't try to run away, Carlin. You wouldn't get far."

Carlin gulped. "Why should I run away? I haven't done a thing. I tell you I'm willing to help all I can. Vic was my friend! I'm sure he was murdered, and—"

Carlin stopped talking. He heard a door close softly. He stood there listening intently, then called the Black Bat's name. Receiving, no answer, he snapped on the lights. The room was empty. He toured the rest of the apartment rapidly, was satisfied that the black-clad intruder was gone, then ran for the photo lab again.

He yanked open a drawer, looked inside, and then leaned weakly against the work-bench. Sweat poured down his face. He quickly removed several photo prints from the drawer and put them into his pocket. He wanted a cigarette and had none, so he hurried to the study. He took a cigarette from a box, raised a lighter with a hand that shook badly. Then he forgot to light the cigarette. That handbag and its contents were gone!

CHAPTER VIII
Lethal Chamber

BUTCH and Carol made their way to the factory town in New Jersey and soon located the big plant of Associated Dyes, Inc. It employed some six hundred people and was working at capacity. These, and other facts, Butch and Carol easily ascertained by having dinner in a cafe not far from the plant.

By pretending to want jobs, they soon made friends with some of the workers. Joel Shea—the "Old Man" who had died a few weeks before—had been held in high regard. The new boss, William B. Wayne, was known to be a stuffed shirt and a driver.

There were, really, two different plants. One had been built five years before the war and the old factory then abandoned and since that time left to rot. It was too far gone even to be repaired for war work.

The new plant was hemmed in by a steel fence, and armed guards patrolled the area. Getting in there would be almost impossible. The old plant, however, was entirely unguarded.

"I've been getting a hunch, Butch," Carol said, after a while. "That fellow who pitched out of the window indicated by such an act that he wasn't free to carry on as an ordinary man would. That meant, to me at least, that he had been hiding out. Maybe in this old plant. Tony especially wants samples of his handwriting and they might be there. I think it's worth a chance."

"Sure," Butch agreed. "No use in our coming all this way for nothing. And you're probably right, because that poor fella's hands were all stained with dyes. He must have been around the plant some place and in the new part they work even nights, so how could he have been there without being seen?"

They made their way toward the deserted building. It was high, but only one story. The darkness hampered them, but Carol did not dare use the flashlight she carried until they were inside the building. Finally they reached the loading platform doors at the rear of the place. Butch examined a large padlock on the door, grinned at Carol and, with one savage wrench, tore the padlock hasps out of the old wood. The door creaked a bit as he pulled it open and the mingled odors of stale chemicals and dust came out to greet them.

Safely within the plant, Carol risked using her flashlight, but their whole project seemed to be hopeless. There was one gigantic room and several smaller ones off it, none of which showed any signs of having been used for years.

Then Carol's flashlight pointed at the edge of an old work-bench. The dust there had been disturbed recently. She threw the beam of the light floorward. The heavy dust had been kicked around a bit and there seemed to be almost a trail formed. It led to a wall, upon which was fixed a large cabinet, like a bookcase, equipped with shelves.

"Look here!" Carol sprayed the floor with the light again. "The cement at this point seems to have been scraped—several times too. Just the barest surface of it. Butch, try to move that cabinet. It should swing out, like a door."

Butch grasped one shelf and tugged. The cabinet did move, with a slight scratching sound across the cement. The whole thing was on hinges. Carol stepped inside the room disclosed. Butch had to bend almost double to enter, the door was so low.

It was a medium-sized room with an unusually high ceiling and rafters. On these rafters was old lumber, and a ladder was propped up so the lumber could be reached if wanted.

"Hey, look!" Butch was using his own flash now. "Somebody lived here. There's a lot of empty cans that had soup and stuff in 'em. Some stale bread and empty soda water bottles. Lots of laboratory things too."

Carol examined the bench. Butch was right—this room had been used as a lab of some kind. Makeshift, perhaps, but in use recently, for a couple of beakers and test tubes still contained unevaporated liquids. There were even two large cylinders of the type used for storing compressed gas, propped in one corner.

Carol laid her handbag on the bench and picked up a large notebook and two smaller ones.

"These must be Victor Shea's notes," she said. "He was hiding out here for some reason, and conducting experiments with dyes. I don't understand the chemical symbols, but I know who will. We're taking these, Butch. Also, see if you can find some samples of writing paper around. To match up with the note Victor wrote."

BUTCH, intent upon searching through several small drawers beneath the bench, struck one of the metal gas cylinders with his shoulder. It must have been delicately balanced for it tipped over, landed on the cement floor and gave off a terrific clanging sound.

Carol shut off her flash instantly. So, did Butch. They stood there, silently listening.

There were stealthy sounds from somewhere in that immense room outside. Carol tip-toed over to Butch and whispered to him:

"We're not alone here and we're trapped in this room! There's only one exit. We're going to climb that ladder and hide on the lumber on the rafters. Easy now—no noise."

Butch went up the ladder first and when Carol reached the top, he took her hand and guided her to a safe perch atop the wide slabs of lumber. They could look straight down at the hidden room.

A momentary flash of light cut the darkness. It came again, this time to stay. The light bobbed crazily as the man who held it bent to get through the low door.

Neither Carol nor Butch could make out the man's identity or even see his form, but he appeared to be almost as excited as they were upon finding this hidden room. The path of his light swept across the bench. Carol's fingers gripped Butch's arms hard.

"My bag," she gasped. "It's on the bench."

They held their breaths, but for once luck seemed to be with them. The handbag was at the far corner of the bench and the intruder centered all his attention upon the part where Victor Shea had worked. He picked up beakers and test tubes, examined bottles of chemicals.

Then he sneezed violently. Carol knew why. She and Butch had dislodged plenty of dust in scrambling over the old boards. It was just sifting down and now probably made a noticeable cloud near the floor.

The intruder suddenly snapped off his flash. For an instant, Carol thought he was ascending the ladder but, instead, it was only the ladder which moved. The man had pulled it down from the rafters. An instant later, they heard a hissing noise, then the scrape of the door and finally there was utter silence.

"He knew we were up here, Butch," Carol said tensely. "He didn't have to see my handbag. The racket that gas cylinder made, and then the dust, told him the whole story. He moved the ladder. We're marooned up here!"

"Maybe he went for help," Butch muttered. "We better think up a good story if the guards from the main plant show up."

"Never mind the story," Carol answered. "I'll be glad if they do come, even if they throw us in the local hoosegow . . . What's that hissing sound?"

"You got me," Butch grunted. "I wonder if any of this lumber is long enough to reach to the floor? I could slide down it."

Carol threw the beam of her flash across the rafters. The lumber fell far short of the considerable distance to the floor of the small room. There was no escape that way. Above them, and well out of reach, was a single skylight.

"Butch," Carol said, "you might use a length of lumber to break out that skylight glass. We're not acrobats, but we might be able to climb up and reach the roof. Anything is better than perching here like a couple of roosters. . . Listen! The door!"

She snapped off the beam of her light and they fell silent. Someone was coming in. The flash bobbed as before when the man crouched to get through the low door. It swept across the room and stopped, directly on Carol's handbag.

The man walked toward it and was suddenly taken with a fit of coughing. They heard a startled exclamation. The man snatched up the handbag and hurried out. The door closed again.

"We're sunk now!" Butch groaned. "And there sure must be a lot of dust floating down. Do you suppose it was the same man who came back?"

"I think so. I . . . Butch! That odor! It's chlorine! One of those cylinders contained compressed chlorine and it's been turned on. No wonder that man coughed so much. Smash that skylight. Quickly! If the stuff fills the room and reaches us, we'll be killed."

Butch worked one length of lumber loose, raised it with those mighty muscles of his and crashed it against the skylight glass. The glass shattered, but the lumber didn't go through.

"There's a grill on the outside," Dutch said disgustedly. "But maybe enough air will come in to keep us from being poisoned."

"Not a chance," Carol told him quietly.

She took his flashlight and hers, turned them both on, and pointed the twin beams straight at the broken skylight.

"Chlorine is a heavy gas," she explained. "It will gradually fill this room, just as water would. When it gets up to our heads, we'll die. That broken skylight only creates a draft which will bring the gas up here faster. If you can pray, Butch start now. Our one and only chance lies in the hope that someone will notice the flashlight beams and come over to investigate."

But Carol knew the weak light would hardly attract any attention. In the first place, the beams would soon fade as the batteries were used. Again, the new factory was too far away.

Butch coughed, a dry, wracking cough. Carol felt her throat go dry. The escaping gas was filling this shaftlike room fast.

Butch took one of the flashlights and threw its beam floorward. They were about eighty feet up, completely stranded. Butch's lower jaw projected aggressively.

"Look!" he said. "I'm a big bozo and I can take all kinds of punishment. If we just stay here, we'll die. Something has to be done—quick."

"No!" Carol cried as she understood Butch's unspoken intention. "If you jump, you may be knocked out, if not killed. Three minutes in that gas-laden atmosphere near the floor and you'll die!"

"I got to take the chance," Butch said quietly. "If I don't get knocked out, I can at least shut off the gas and open the door even if I bust both my legs in the jump. It's got to be done. Or have you any other ideas?"

"If we only had some rope!" Carol cried. "Or if that murderer hadn't guessed we were up here and moved the ladder."

"How long before this stuff will get us?" Butch asked.

"Perhaps twenty minutes more—or half an hour at the most. We're just getting wisps of it so far."

"I'll wait until we can hardly stand it," Butch said resolutely. "Then I'm going to jump. And don't try to talk me out of it."

CHAPTER IX
Footprints for Two

HASTILY the Black Bat left Carlin's apartment house, moving as swiftly as he could travel, taking great risks of being seen,

The Black Bat gave Buckley a tremendous yank as the heavy branch came crashing down
(CHAPTER X)

15

with only the wide-brimmed hat for protection. The hood was safely tucked away in his pocket.

When he reached the car he drove as fast as he dare. Carol and Butch were in trouble! Undoubtedly, they were at the plant, perhaps prisoners and in serious danger. The fact that Carlin had been in possession of Carol's handbag was significant.

The factory was not far across the river and fortunately traffic was light, so the Black Bat traveled fast. He had already studied the location of the plan on maps and knew precisely where he was going.

As he came within sight of the sprawling factory, he braked the car gradually. The place was brightly lighted, and he began to feel a bit easier. How could anything happen here, with so many people about?"

Then he caught sight of the old factory, and saw the faint beam of light that projected through the skylight. With the rest of the big place shrouded by darkness, that meant something. He parked the car, drew on his hood and started moving rapidly in the direction of the building.

That faint beacon drew him like a magnet. He found the broken hasps on the loading platform doors and recognized this as Butch's work. He hurried into the plant and his uncanny eyes penetrated the darkness. He listened, heard no sound, then his nostrils twitched. The easily recognizable odor of chlorine had reached him.

He broke out in a cold sweat. Chlorine was synonymous with death, and Carol and Butch were in here somewhere!

He followed this invisible trail as the gas grew stronger and stronger. Soon he knew it came from beneath what seemed to be just solid wall. He rapped hard on the wall. Faintly, he heard someone shout.

The Black Bat looked for the hidden entrance and his abnormal sight saw things that Carol and Butch had missed. Smudges on the shelves of the cabinet were proof that they had been grasped hard. He pulled the cabinet back. Chlorine came out in a violent gust. Covering his mouth and nose, he darted into the room, and took in the situation with one sweeping glance.

He quickly propped the ladder back where it had been, then fled for fresher air. When he returned, Carol was down the ladder—and had dropped to the floor—clinging to the rungs of the ladder weakly. The Black Bat swung her into his arms and hurried out of the room. Butch followed, reeling a bit, and grinning from ear to ear. He clutched the note-books which Carol had found.

Fresh air revived them fairly well. Then the Black Bat headed his car back to the city while Carol told the story.

"Victor Shea lived and worked in that room all right," she declared. "We've evidence of that, I think. Someone else came there tonight, probably in an attempt to find what Butch and I stumbled upon. Whoever it was heard the clatter of the gas cylinder when it fell. He saw my handbag on the bench the second time he came into that room."

"But he turned on the gas cylinder the first time," the Black Bat said. "Why, then, would he come back for another look, knowing the gas must be filling that room fairly fast? Are you certain it was the same man?"

"We couldn't see his face or even his form," Carol explained, "because both times he was bent over so he could get through the low doorway."

The Black Bat said nothing for moments while he thought.

"There were two men, Carol," he said then. "Both so tall they had to crouch to enter the doorway. I had to duck slightly myself, but I also noticed two sets of footprints in the dust, overlapping your small shoes and Butch's gunboats. One man wore rubber heels, the other leather. Now, we have a little group of suspects. Of them, only two men are so tall that they would have to crouch to get through that door. Attorney Donald Buckley and Felix Carlin. I happen to know that Carlin was one of them."

"But how in the world could you know that?" Butch asked.

The Black Bat took Carol's handbag from the seat beside him and placed it in her lap. "I was in Carlin's apartment when he returned, and he had your purse, Carol," he said.

Then Carlin must be your man!" Carol said quickly.

"If there was only a motive, yes," the Black Bat agreed. "But Carlin can't profit from any of this. He was just Victor Shea's friend. He's the one man we really have evidence on, but he has no motive, and until we find one, we can't take action against him. Remember also—someone besides Carlin was in that room. The first man, the one who turned on the gas cylinder. He didn't know who was hiding on the rafters, but he didn't care. Carlin popped in shortly after, saw your handbag and got out because the chlorine drove him away."

THEY were getting close to Tony Quinn's house now. The Black Bat drove the car to the curb.

"Butch," he instructed, "go into that store across the street and tele-phone Silk. Tell him we're ready to enter the lab and that he is to keep McGrath's detectives occupied for the next ten minutes. Then you'd better go home for some rest. That gas hasn't done you any good."

Butch nodded. "I do feel a little shaky, I guess. Okay—I'll signal after I phone Silk." Within the next ten minutes Carol and the Black Bat had safely reached the privacy and the security of the lab. There the Black Bat stripped off his somber clothing and became Tony Quinn once more. He sat down at the lab bench, examined the notes which Carol and Butch had found, and whistled sharply.

"You really found something, Carol," he declared. "Victor Shea had probably conducted certain experiments in the factory labs, then gone into hiding for some reason we don't know yet. He brought along the chemicals and apparatus necessary to continue his work—and he finished it. He was working on new types of dyes which will be used for nylon and glass-spun cloth after the war."

Carol nodded slowly. "Worth a lot of money too, I expect. I think we'll also find that Lyle Alexander, the chemist for Associated Dyes, was trying to discover the same thing. If Shea beat him to it, Alexander would lose out. So he has an excellent motive for killing him."

"And that," Quinn acknowledged, "makes sense, because Alexander's hands were similarly stained—with the same colors and in the same intensity as the stains on Victor Shea's hands. These new dyes are peculiar in that they must be fast dyes and the stains couldn't be removed from the hands. Regular dyes can be washed off with certain solvents."

"Then,"—Carol spread her hands in a gesture of finality—"you have your killer."

Quinn laughed. "Without a shred of evidence beyond a motive. And don't forget that Alexander is a short, bulky individual. He doesn't answer the descriptions furnished by the two men who were hired to kill me. The accent in one case was on an average appearing man; in the other, a tall man. Alexander can't fill the bill. And then we have Carlin whom we know is mixed up in it."

"Carlin has no motive," Carol said musingly.

"That we know of," Quinn amended. "Don't forget that William Wayne seems to dislike Carlin heartily. Of course the knife was Carlin's. He stole your handbag and made no attempt to find out if the escaping chlorine was directed at anyone. In fact, there is even the possibility that he turned it on, forgot to take your bag the first time and returned for it. Despite the two sets of shoe prints, that can be true."

Carol sighed deeply. "Then where have we progressed, Tony? Everything is just the same as before. Motives and clues, but they seem to be directed toward no one man."

"True," Quinn agreed. "So it is necessary for us to find further clues. Motives also, if there are any."

Silk entered the lab and ended further discussion.

"There was a phone call about half an hour ago, sir," he said. "From Attorney Buckley. He wants you to come out to his Long Island home and see him. It's vitally important, he said, and he is afraid to come here. Sounds phony to me, sir."

Quinn frowned. "It does have a false ring. Just the same, we'll go and see him. Not quite as he expects though. How about the detectives? Are they set for the night?"

"Fed and pampered." Silk smiled.

"We'll give them more peace and quiet," Quinn said. "Tell them you and I are going out on an important mission, but that they should continue to watch the house. Then bring the car around to the front. Tony Quinn is going to visit Attorney Buckley at his home, but the trip is going to take a little longer than actually necessary, for somewhere on the way the Black Bat is going to pass our car and reach Buckley's home first. Carol, you stay here and keep tabs on the phone. Be sure McGrath's detectives don't see you."

Silk was stepping out of the lab when Quinn called him to a halt.

"Silk," he instructed, "when you go into the garage, stow a couple of shovels in the car. Where they can't be seen."

"Shovels, sir?" Silk asked, with a questioning expression.

"That's right. You and I, Silk, are going to be a combination of burglar and ghoul tonight."

Shortly afterwards, Silk pulled up in front of the house, got out, and went to escort Tony Quinn to the car.

The two detectives were close by, but a coat covered the black clothing of the Black Bat, which Quinn wore over his usual gray tweeds.

Silk started off on the fairly long drive to Buckley's Long Island home. It was several miles from where William B. Wayne lived.

CHAPTER X
Death from Above

NEARING Buckley's home, Tony Quinn removed his topcoat, donned black gloves and the hood, and gave Silk certain instructions. They checked their watches so that they agreed perfectly. Then the Black Bat slipped off in the darkness.

He didn't intend to visit Buckley's estate by orthodox methods. This whole thing might be a sort of scheme to finish off Tony Quinn and such a suspicion called for a careful examination of the premises first.

The Black Bat cut across the rear of an adjoining estate. His strange vision served him very well for it was a dark night, and anyone possessed of only ordinary sight would have found the going difficult.

Buckley's house was big, and his estate covered fully two acres. House and grounds were enclosed by a neat white fence with a gate in front. Visitors were required to walk along a rather narrow, pretty and winding path from the road to the house.

The Black Bat, crouched in the darkness, thought it over. If a trap had been prepared for Tony Quinn, it wouldn't be obvious because although Quinn was apparently blind, he would have someone with him who could see. Also the trap would have to be set somewhere outside the house so that even if Buckley was behind it, he could claim that another person had arranged the thing.

The Black Bat proceeded along the fence until he reached the path. He started down it, watching and listening carefully. He made no sound for he kept on the grass bordering the path. If it was planned for something to happen to the blind D. A. it would be, he reasoned, something which could be construed as an accident. Nothing quite so blatant as a gunman hidden in the brush waiting to open fire.

Then across the path he saw a thin black cord, completely invisible to average eyes. It was about ankle-high and anyone walking was bound to hit it. The Black Bat examined the set-up carefully. Something was to happen when that cord was tripped. He discovered that the cord was strung beneath the branch of a bush and disappeared somewhere above, among the leaves of a large oak.

Standing directly beneath the tree, the Black Bat penetrated the darkness with his keen eyesight and saw all details of the trick. A large and heavy branch was delicately balanced high in the tree, so arranged that it would fall if the cord across the path were tripped. The tree trunk was tall, and bare of branches which might check the descent of the murder weapon.

It was a neat, competently constructed trap. The murderer had only to remove the cord after the crime was committed and all traces of murder would be gone. Branches of old trees were bound to fall occasionally and this, unfortunately, would hit and either kill or badly maim a blind Special District Attorney and his guide.

The Black Bat skirted the path, circled the house, and found the back door easy to open. There would be servants, so he took all precautions. He had noticed a light in one of the upstairs rooms and he made his way through the house, in that direction. Here again, darkness meant nothing and, unfamiliar as the place was, he stumbled against no furniture and made no more noise than a cat on the prowl.

He found the door of the lighted room open and Attorney Buckley was in there, quietly reading. He wore a smoking jacket over a sport shirt and sport trousers. The Black Bat drew his gun and stepped into the room.

Buckley was a strange type of man. Even the sudden appearance of the Black Bat broke his usual calm only to the degree of making him blink a few times, as if this somberly dressed man was an apparition that would at once dissolve into thin air.

"Good evening," the Black Bat said conversationally. "I'm sorry to intrude this way, but I don't usually announce my presence by ringing the doorbell."

"Um—so I've heard." Buckley laid his book down on an end table, leaned back, and crossed his legs.

He seemed to be entirely at ease, but the Black Bat could see that a vein in the attorney's throat was throbbing. His calm was purely exterior.

"You're interested in the Shea matter, aren't you?" Buckley asked.

THE Black Bat sat down, but his gun was still trained on Buckley.

"I think Victor Shea was murdered," he said. "All murders interest me. I'm looking for motives, and you're the man to tell me about one. Would William Wayne have inherited Joel Shea's estate if Victor had lived?"

"Yes," Buckley said. "I'm going to be honest with you. Frankly, I trust neither the police nor Quinn, the Special D.A. Oh, I know his reputation of honesty, but reputations are always good—before they go bad. Joel Shea liked both his grandsons, but Victor much more than William. Joel started a dye manufacturing business, built it up to a large and profitable enterprise, and hoped that Victor would some day take over."

"William wasn't expected to assume any important position in the plant?" the Black Bat asked.

"Of course he was. Victor, however, had a scientific bent. He was a good chemist but, unfortunately, he also had a palate for alcohol. He liked to gamble and, in short, he broke the old man's heart."

"So Victor was disinherited?"

"Exactly—but with certain provisions. Victor was working on a new type of dye. I don't pretend to understand it, but the job seemed difficult and called for intensive work and long hours. Joel provided that if Victor completed his work before he died, then Victor was to have the estate. If not, it all went to William Wayne."

"Victor did complete his experiments," the Black Bat said quietly. "There is evidence of that."

"But Victor is dead and in that event the property was to go to Wayne anyhow. Do you think Wayne killed Victor to get possession of the estate. I don't."

"Well, at least," the Black Bat said, "I have no evidence of it so far. What do you know about Lyle Alexander? Wouldn't he be jealous of Victor if he discovered the new dye first?"

"He was always jealous of him. Victor was the better chemist of the two even if Alexander held the title of chief chemist for the firm. If Alexander discovered the dye, patented it, he would make a lot of money."

"And Mr. Carlin, who is a friend of the family. What of him?"

Buckley's face went grim and dark. "I'd rather not talk about Carlin. He's a—cad. That's putting it mildly. Also, I might add that I firmly believe Victor committed suicide. He did not know his grandfather's estate would be his if he succeeded with the dye. He thought it had all gone to William. And Victor seemed to have been a bit unbalanced mentally."

"Any specific reasons for saying that?" the Black Bat asked.

Buckley nodded. "At the old man's funeral, I saw Victor bend over the casket covertly. He had a tiny pair of scissors in his hand and he snipped some of the old man's hair off, and the nail tips from two fingers. Rather macabre mementos, don't you think?"

"Did anyone else see him do that?"

"I don't believe so. He was clever about it. Of course, the others were all present. Someone may have seen it."

"And you have nothing further to tell me?" the Black Bat asked.

"Nothing—right now," Buckley answered slowly. "Later I might. . . But then I'm not so certain. At any rate, it has no direct connection with the death of Victor Shea."

The Black Bat arose. "Mr. Buckley, I'm going to ask you to walk with me to the gate. Do you mind?"

Buckley attempted a weak smile. "Why, of course not, but I never did hear of the Black Bat being escorted out of a house, any more than he is escorted in. I'll go, though. Let me get my hat and coat."

They were careful not to awaken the servants. Outside, the Black Bat walked beside Buckley, his shoulder brushing the attorney's so that he could feel the slightest slow-down on Buckley's part. If he knew about that trap, he would never spring it because the thing was almost certain death.

The fine black and invisible cord was five feet ahead of them and still Buckley kept on approaching, without the slightest lag. His right foot moved out, encountered the trip cord, and the Black Bat suddenly gave Buckley a tremendous yank. It carried them both out of the way as the heavy branch came crashing down.

Buckley, flat on the ground now, turned deathly pale.

"What on earth?" he choked.

"Odd wasn't it, how a branch would fall at this particular moment?" the Black Bat said dryly. "Seems as if the thing was set to fall, but I'm positive of this, Buckley. If that was a method of murder, you had nothing to do with it. Murderers don't risk their own lives, springing their own traps. Good night, Mr. Buckley."

SWIFTLY the Black Bat faded into the darkness. Buckley arose, walked over and shuddered as he saw what the branch had done to the path. There were great holes gouged in it. He studied the scene for a few more minutes, was about to turn back then paused. A car was coming down the street slowly as if the driver was searching for the correct address.

It stopped. Buckley went to the gate. He saw Silk open the car door and help Tony Quinn to alight. Buckley made a wry face at sight of the blind man. As Silk and Quinn reached the gate, Buckley stepped into view. Silk came to an abrupt halt, dragging Quinn back and speaking to him in a low voice.

"What do you want?" Buckley demanded. "It's I—Attorney Buckley. I never expected to see you here tonight, Quinn."

"You didn't expect me?" Quinn said, in a puzzled voice. "But you phoned my home and asked me to come here on a matter of considerable importance. You acted as if you were afraid to leave your own house. That's the only reason I came."

Buckley opened his mouth to make an angry retort. Then he turned and looked back at the path where the limb had crashed. His eyes grew wider. If Quinn had been lured here it was with the idea of making him the victim of that falling limb.

"Just how much do you want, Quinn?" Buckley said. "A final figure."

"I don't seem to understand," Quinn answered. "I don't want anything, beyond the possible murderer of Victor Shea. I thought you asked me here so you could tell me something important."

Buckley removed his hat and ran fingers through his gray hair.

"Never mind what I said about an offer. I may be wrong. Dead wrong! However, I did not telephone you, Mr. Quinn. There is no reason why I should want to see you."

"Someone must have been playing jokes," Quinn said nervously. "I'm sorry, Mr. Buckley. Take me home again, Silk."

Buckley eyed the retreating figure and again glanced at the fallen limb. He shook his head from side to side like a sorely perplexed man.

CHAPTER XI
Murder Needs a Motive

IN the car, Tony Quinn chuckled.

"That worked beautifully," he told Silk. "Buckley hasn't the faintest idea that the Black Bat merely cut across lots, popped into his car and returned as Tony Quinn. It was a trap, Silk, but Buckley didn't set it because I gave him the opportunity to spring the thing and he showed no anxiety."

"But what did he mean by asking you how much you wanted?"

Quinn laughed aloud. "The good Attorney Buckley thinks I'm blackmailing him. Or, rather, one of his clients. I can't have such a reputation as that, so we'll proceed to clean it up. Head for Fairview Cemetery, Silk."

Before Silk could express his surprise at this order, Quinn talked to him softly for a few minutes. They drove on to the graveyard then, where they spent the better part of an hour.

"Now where?" Silk asked when they were back in the car.

"The home of William B. Wayne. I want to see what sort of a reception the Black Bat will get from him. Park this side of his house and grounds. I'll look the place over before I make myself known. Also to make certain there aren't any more of those smart traps, like the one at Buckley's."

"I wonder why they want to kill Tony Quinn?" Silk asked uneasily. "There's no reason for it. Suppose Victor Shea did write a letter and leave it at the house. If you'd got it, the murderer would be behind bars by now. He isn't, so why can't he realize there either wasn't such a letter written or that someone else got it?"

"Maybe,"—the Black Bat chuckled—"the someone else who did get it isn't mentioning the fact, and the murderer thinks I'm playing a little game of my own. At any rate, it really doesn't matter. Tomorrow I'll compel the killer to reveal himself—and don't ask questions, because I'm not posi-tive as to his identity yet."

Silk pulled the car off the road, beneath some overhanging branches. They were about an eighth of a mile from William Wayne's handsome old home which he, however, had but recently acquired. The Black Bat started to get out of the car, but quickly ducked back inside again. A motor was roaring as its driver pushed it to the limit. The car, without lights, sped crazily up the road in their direction. The Black Bat watched it, swung his body to follow it as the vehicle flashed by.

"That," he said slowly, "was Felix Carlin, traveling as if all the assorted devils in Hades were after him. He came from Wayne's place too. There's been trouble there!"

He sped toward the house, a hardly visible shadow in the night. Lights were on all over the first floor. Through a window he could see servants moving about excitedly. The Black Bat walked boldly onto the porch, but didn't announce himself by ringing the bell. The door was half-open so he merely walked inside, but he did take the precaution of drawing his gun.

In the living room he found William Wayne lying on a divan, while two servants mopped blood off his face and another was trying to straighten the room a bit. The room looked as if a long and serious battle had gone on in it.

"There's no reason to be alarmed," the Black Bat said when a servant spotted him and gaped in apprehension so great he couldn't speak. "I'm the Black Bat. What happened here?"

Wayne struggled into a sitting position, took a wet cloth from one servant and ministered to himself. He ordered the servants out of the room.

"Please don't call the police," the Black Bat told them. "I'm here only to help Mr. Wayne."

"The only help I need," Wayne said, "is for someone to throw Felix Carlin within range of my fists. I've changed my mind about Victor's death. I think Carlin murdered him!"

"Why?" the Black Bat queried.

"He came here tonight and told me he could take over the firm, or bankrupt it, whichever he chose. He gave no reasons, but I'm afraid that Victor owed him a great deal of money and Carlin thinks I'm going to pay off his debts."

"Again I ask, why?" the Black Bat said.

WAYNE went over and poured himself a drink. Gripping the glass so hard that his knuckles gleamed he turned to face the intruder in black.

"Because Carlin knows darn well I'll pay up to avoid any kind of family scandal. Victor must have been in a peck of trouble. Frankly, Carlin demanded ten thousand dollars from me upon threat of exposing some sordid affair. It can concern only Victor. Certainly I've never stepped off the straight and narrow."

"How does it happen you're beaten up, Mr. Wayne?"

"I started to throw Carlin out and he produced a gun. Before he could level it, I charged him and he used the weapon as a blackjack. The man is mad! He said he'd beat my brains out—and he was doing a pretty good job of it too before I yelled for help. Then Carlin just ran out and fled."

"It appears to be a matter for the police," the Black Bat suggested. "Why not call Tony Quinn and give him the facts?"

"Quinn?" Wayne howled. "If anything, he works hand in glove with Carlin! He must be doing that, for Carlin actually boasted that I couldn't touch him. Said that Quinn would protect him and punish me. My attorney agrees. He doesn't trust Quinn either."

"Too bad," the Black Bat said. "Quinn's reputation has been perfect up to now. I rather like the fellow. Perhaps you're wrong. Carlin could have conjured up a lie to make you fear him more."

"I wouldn't put it past him," Wayne grumbled. "Why did you come here? Are you interested in this—this ghastly pack of trouble?"

"Very much so, Mr. Wayne. I came to ask a few questions, but I feel that you've undergone enough for the present. Therefore I won't press you, except for one thing. Has your chief chemist, Lyle Alexander, brought forth any new dye substances lately? Something that could be worth a great deal of money."

"Not yet," Wayne replied. "He's working in a few things right now. If they pan out he'll make a mint of money. So will I. Why should that interest you?"

"It's possible that murder has been

done, and murder needs a motive. Alexander supplies one—perhaps. I'll be back, Mr. Wayne, when things are more normal here, and you have your wits about you. Perhaps we can think of a way to expose Carlin, for instance."

Wayne shrugged. "I'll do anything you say, but Carlin is no fool. He'll be protected in half a dozen different ways. Thanks, anyhow, for not pressing me to-night. I really do feel the effects of that argument."

The Black Bat nodded, stepped through the door and closed it.

When Wayne reached the hallway, there were no signs of the black-clad visitor. Wayne went upstairs to cleanse his lacerations better. At least that was what he informed his servants. But five minutes later he had slipped out of the house, taken a car from the garage, and was driving toward the skylighted horizon that was New York.

Silk saw the car flash by and broke out in a cold sweat of worry until the Black Bat appeared. The Black Bat had a small package under one arm, and he was chuckling in vast satisfaction. . . .

At nine-thirty the next morning, Tony Quinn's car pulled up in front of William Wayne's house. Quinn got out and, under Silk's guidance moved to the porch and waited for someone to answer Silk's ring. A servant opened the door. Quinn went in and Wayne greeted him sourly.

"I got your phone call," Wayne said. "I waited as you ordered me to. It must be nice to have authority and

exercise it whenever you wish. Why should I wait for you? I'm a busy man."

"Undoubtedly," Quinn said gently. "So am I—and my work is concerned with murder. Truthfully, Mr. Wayne, I'm taking you to my office shortly. You'll have to come. Otherwise I'll be compelled to send police out here after you."

"I guess you can do that," Wayne grumbled. "Well, do we start now?"

"First, I want to talk to you," Quinn told him. "It so happens that my man has business elsewhere. Will you drive me into town, Mr. Wayne? Thanks. I knew you would . . . All right, Silk. You can report to the office after you have completed the errand I outlined."

SILK hurried out of the house and drove away. Tony Quinn rumbled around a bit until Wayne helped him over to a chair. Quinn's eyes were the eyes of a blind man, focused on nothing. His head was turned well to the left of the spot where Wayne sat down.

"Last night," Quinn said, "I was summoned to the home of your attorney. A strange summons because it was in Buckley's name and he denied calling me. At any rate, Buckley seemed decidedly antagonistic to me. He made several odd statements. Now he is acting solely as your attorney, so I came to you. What's wrong?"

"I don't know what you're talking about," Wayne snapped. "I'm tired of being questioned. If Buckley has anything against you, it's his business, not mine."

"Very well," Quinn said meekly. "Will you give me a hand? I'm ready to go."

Wayne was morosely silent as he drove toward the main highway leading to the tunnel and the city. Once his foot came down on the brake hard and he uttered an exclamation, but shrugged off Quinn's polite inquiry until they were in the neighborhood of Quinn's office. Then Wayne spoke.

"You may have felt the car slow down a little while ago. I was passing the cemetery where my grandfather and Victor are buried. I noticed that the graves seemed to have been freshly dug up. Has there been an exhumation?"

"Why, not to my knowledge." Quinn seemed greatly surprised.

"I didn't ask for such an order. Perhaps Captain McGrath will know something about it. He'll be at my office. So will everyone else involved."

CHAPTER XII
Murder and Blackmail

WAYNE found a place to park, aided Quinn in alighting and took his arm to guide him through the pedestrian traffic, which was heavy. They entered the doorway of the huge civic building.

"It is my growing conviction," Quinn said, "that your cousin did commit suicide. I may throw the whole affair out of my office when this meeting is over. There is a sad lack of evidence."

"I always said it was suicide," Wayne snapped. He propelled Quinn into one of the elevators. "However, I'm glad to learn that you are finally being reasonable."

He gave the number of Quinn's floor to the elevator operator and said nothing more during the trip up. He helped Quinn out and led him along the corridor, turned to the left, and walked toward Quinn's office.

"I can't for the life of me understand why you want us all in the office this morning," he grumbled. "I hope you'll be brief about it. Factories—big ones like mine—don't run themselves, you know."

He opened the door and Captain McGrath came forward to take Quinn's arm. The others had arrived. Carlin glared at Wayne from his slumped position in a big leather chair. Attorney Buckley just nodded curtly. Lyle Alexander, the chemist, seemed intent upon trying to pare some of the dyestuff from beneath his fingernails. He didn't raise his head or acknowledge the arrival of his boss in any way.

Quinn sat down at his desk.

"Is everybody here?" he asked.

"Alexander, Buckley, Carlin—and you brought along Wayne," McGrath replied. "That accounts for them all. I've got the two mugs in the next room too."

"Good," Quinn said. "Gentlemen, for some reason I can't fathom there have been deliberate attempts made on my life. In one instant a man was hired to come to this office and murder me. But I haven't been alone as a victim. Last night the Black Bat visited me. He also had been attacked by a paid assassin. The hoodlums responsible have been under arrest since. They will be brought in here."

"To identify us?" Carlin shouted and jumped to his feet. "That's an outrage! If we're charged with something, put us under arrest!"

"Take it easy," McGrath said, "or I'll oblige you. Okay, Mr. Quinn to bring those mugs in?"

"Line these four men up first," Quinn ordered. "And any of them who refuses will automatically come under heavy suspicion. Innocent men are not afraid."

The four lined up. McGrath brought in the hophead first. He was shaking badly and seemed eager to get this over with. He walked straight up to Carlin and pressed a finger against his chest.

"That s him!"

"You're a liar!" Carlin shrieked. "I never saw this man before in my life."

The other man entered, studied the quartette and repeated the hophead's maneuver. Carlin was sweating profusely by this time. He staggered over to a chair and literally fell into it. Alexander was smiling smugly. Buckley just looked astonished and Wayne's features were frozen into what seemed to be deep anxiety.

Quinn took the razor-keen knife from the drawer of his desk.

"I think this is your property, Mr. Carlin. It was used in an attempt to murder the Black Bat. He tells me a scabbard into which this blade fits is in your apartment."

"Certainly that's my knife," Carlin groaned. "It was stolen from me days ago. I tell you I'm innocent! Give me a break!"

"I imagine," Quinn said ironically, "that many of your victims have begged you in those same words— 'Give me a break.' What was your answer to them?"

"You—you've got me mixed up with someone else!" Carlin shouted. "I don't even know what you're talking about."

"You're a professional blackmailer," Quinn said coldly. "You prey on the mistakes people make. You get hold of documents that can ruin a man, then photostat them . . . Captain McGrath, didn't you say Carlin's apartment was equipped for photostating papers?"

"I'll say it was," McGrath grunted. "We found a few prints too, checked on the people involved, and some of them are ready to testify against him."

"It's a framed-up plan to keep me quiet!" Carlin shouted. "But I won't be silent. I demand protection!"

William Wayne stepped forward.

"Quinn," he said, if Carlin is criminally involved in something, I intend to help him. Therefore, keep in mind that Attorney Buckley and myself are on his side. After all, Carlin is a family friend."

"And he knows a great deal," Quinn said calmly. "Let me tell you what I know. Victor Shea was murdered—by someone in this room who tricked him into that office upstairs. Shea tried to bargain for his life by saying he had left a letter at my home, just in case he was prevented from reaching me. The murderer had to get that letter, but Carlin beat him to it. Carlin knew what was going on. Probably he helped Victor hide out. He trailed Victor, saw him deposit his letter at my home, and Carlin got it. He has been blackmailing the murderer."

Carlin gulped, looked around, but decided there wasn't much hope for an escape.

"The Black Bat has been working on this," Quinn went on. "Most of what I know came from his lips. The murderer went to my home and didn't find the letter. He became alarmed, believed I had it and was withholding action. So he tried to kill me—with a bullet the first time and then, because of the risk, he hired a man to do the job. He retained another paid assassin to seize Carlin if he went to the morgue and identified Victor, but the killer was lured into a trap by the Black Bat. Both these killers described the man who retained them. Their descriptions fitted Carlin and they even identified him a few moments ago."

"But I never saw those men before in my life!" Carlin shrieked.

"Of course you didn't," Quinn conceded. "The murderer was building up a case against you. He needed a weapon at one time so he took your ornamental letter opener, sharpened it and turned it into a dangerous dagger. By your own actions, in conducting this blackmailing scheme, you built up more suspicion against your-

self. You pretended that I was working with you to frighten the murderer even more."

Wayne suddenly stepped away from Attorney Buckley. "If—if a murderer was trying to throw blame on Carlin he must have had a build like Carlin's. Buckley is just as tall."

Buckley's eyes narrowed, but he said nothing. Tony Quinn apparently noticed none of this. His blind eyes were just as blank as ever.

"Who is the man you were blackmailing, Carlin?" he asked softly.

Carlin licked his lips. "I—I don't know anything about it. I —I don't even think Victor was murdered. There's some mistake."

"I thought you wouldn't talk," Quinn said. "In holding back your information, you can force the murderer to help you."

"Good heavens!" cried Wayne, in a startled voice. "I hope you don't think I was trying to shut him up by my offer to aid him. It just seemed like the right thing to do."

Quinn apparently paid no attention to Wayne's entreaty.

"Victor went into hiding because he was afraid of being murdered," he said. "He had to finish a certain set of experiments in a hurry, for unless he did, his grandfather would leave him nothing. By the same token the killer had to work fast and kill Victor before he completed his work. Only he couldn't find him.

"Victor knew his grandfather had been murdered. He took the cuttings of the dead man's hair and fingernails. We can therefore assume, since

Victor was a chemist, and would know that the grandfather was killed by arsenic, which shows itself even after death in the hair and nails of the victim. It can also be used without suspicious results on an old and ailing man like Joel Shea.

"Finally, Victor finished his work. He came out of hiding and tried to get in touch with me so he could tell his story and furnish the proof that his grandfather was murdered and that he, himself was in great danger. He never got the chance. Somehow, our killer found him. Wayne—you're the murderer. You killed the old man so you'd inherit. If he lived until Victor finished his experiments, you'd get nothing. Then you had to kill Victor to protect yourself."

Wayne drew himself up. "I'm afraid you will have to prove that, Mr. Quinn."

Quinn nodded. "I expect to. Once I do, Carlin will realize you can no longer help him and he will talk to save himself. Buckley, you're innocent of any part, but you will admit that you believed Carlin and I were working hand in glove to blackmail Wayne."

"Yes, I did," Buckley confessed. "I thought it was something about Victor's past life—the family reputation. Carlin kept hinting that he knew you well. Now I see that it was only to impress Wayne with the idea that Victor's letter to you was in existence and to compel Wayne to pay out heavy sums."

"He did pay twenty-five thousand," Quinn said. "The Black Bat dis-

covered evidence of that. Wayne, thinking I was trying to profit, was all the more determined to kill me. Some of his tricks were clever. As for the difference in appearance between Carlin and Wayne that could be easily arranged. Carlin's loud clothes may not be in the best of taste, but all stores sell them. Wayne hoped that Victor might go to a grave as an unidentified suicide. Printing Victor's picture smoked him out, of course . . . Captain, you'd better handcuff Wayne. I can't see him, but I imagine he is growing more and more desperate."

"Desperate, my hat!" Wayne replied tartly. "What you've told so far doesn't mean a thing."

THE handcuffs were put on, nevertheless.

Someone tapped on the office door. McGrath opened it and Silk walked in, carrying a package and wearing a broad grin.

"As you ordered, sir," he told Quinn, "I returned to Mr. Wayne's home after he left. I searched it and found a pair of built-up shoes. I imagine they add enough height to compare with Carlin's size. And, in the cellar, I found a sharpening stone. It had been recently used and there were tiny dust particles which I'm sure will match the metal from which Carlin's dagger is made."

Wayne tried to bolt. He had taken about four steps when McGrath grabbed him. Wayne sank into a chair, his face deathly white.

"Last night," Quinn said, "the Black

Bat dug up the surface of Joel Shea's grave. This morning Wayne noticed it on his way to the office with me. He betrayed his anxiety over a post-mortem by almost stopping the car. He realized he had practically given himself away so he attempted to bluster it out by asking me if I'd ordered such a post-mortem. I hadn't, naturally, because I'd never thought of it or had sufficient cause to get a legal order. Now I shall take the necessary steps.

"But even if we had little evidence against Mr. Wayne, I'm afraid he gave himself away when he brought me into this building . . . Carlin—Alexander—Buckley, all of you went to the wrong office, didn't you?"

There was a chorus of assents.

"The lobby listing was wrong" Buckley said. "It indicated your office was on the eighteenth floor."

Quinn smiled. "None of you, including Wayne, had ever been to my office before—at least openly. Wayne lured Victor into the wrong office by switching the room numbers on the lobby listing. I left them that way. Today I kept Mr. Wayne busy talking, excited over the grave that seemed to have been opened. He didn't stop to think, but I'm a blind man so I couldn't direct Wayne. He didn't look at the listing, because we were walking too fast. The names and numbers are in small letters. Nevertheless, Wayne brought me straight to this office because he knew where it was. He had to check that in order to arrange the false listing which trapped Victor. Carlin—how about it?"

Carlin sighed. "At least I'm no killer, and Wayne did try to have me murdered if what you say is the truth. I thought I was being followed and I was afraid to go to the morgue and identify Victor. Yes, I have the letter Vic wrote you. I'm sunk, so I'll salvage what I can. Wayne killed him. I did try to build up the idea that you were working with me so I could get more money out of him. I should have known better—especially after the Black Bat showed up. I knew where Victor was hiding in the old factory too. I trailed him that night he first went there."

Wayne looked up, all hope gone. "I should have killed you first," he muttered to Carlin.

McGrath called in his men. Wayne and Carlin were removed, and gradually the office was cleared. McGrath lit a cigar, studied the tip of it intently.

"Funny how the Black Bat stayed so low in this matter," he said musingly. "Now I fully expected him to show up today, and I took certain precautions to trap him. Men posted all around. But maybe they were seen. Of course, not by you, Quinn. You're totally blind. Yet you do accomplish some smooth investigations. Too smooth, if you ask me."

Quinn grinned. "Are you never satisfied, Captain? You have your murderer, a blackmailer, and all the credit you want. This work wasn't mine. The Black Bat accomplished it, turning his information over to me last night. Naturally, I can't say it was my work. I can't admit the Black Bat is all but on my staff. So you accept the glory. Is anything fairer than that?"

McGrath took a long breath and arose.

"Oh, what's the use?" he grumbled. At the door he turned for a moment. "Just the same I'm glad I did help a little. If I hadn't posted those men, you might be a corpse right now. Sullivan told me how that acid barrel almost finished you off, how helpless you were when the thing started rolling."

Quinn's face lit up.

"More evidence that I'm blind and I couldn't be the Black Bat, Captain. Now will you believe me?"

Captain McGrath bit all the way through his cigar.

THE END

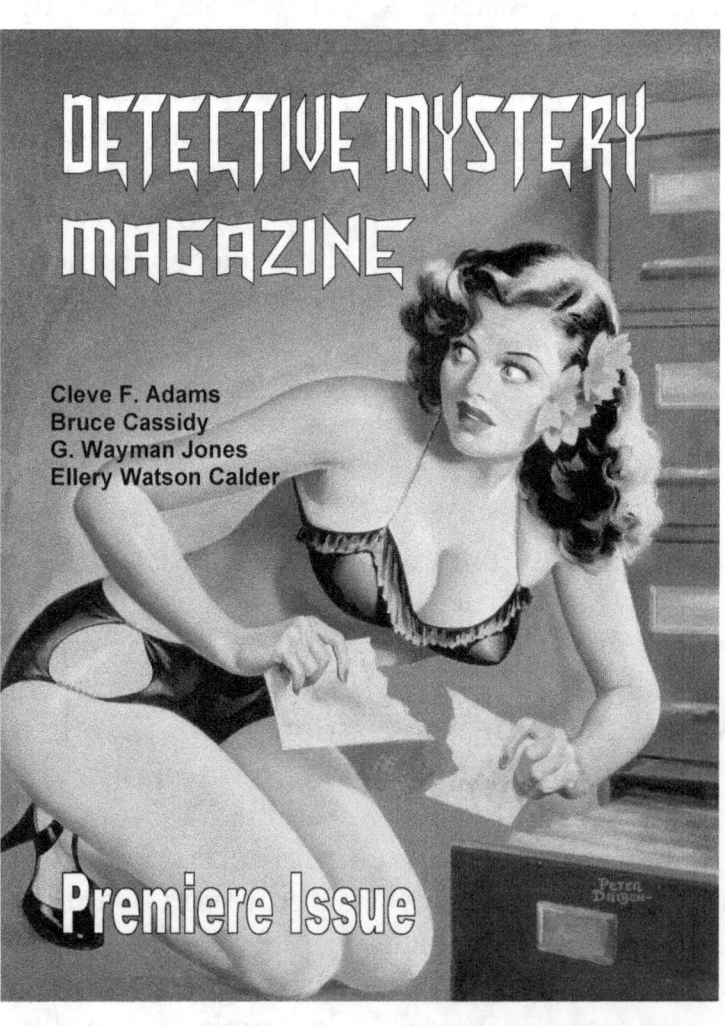

www.ingramcontent.com/pod-product-compliance
Lightning Source LLC
Chambersburg PA
CBHW080817250626
47159CB00010B/3422